nickelodeon

BIG NATE

PRANK YOU VERY MUCH

Inspired by the comics and
book series by Lincoln Peirce

Based on the episodes written by
Sarah Allan, Mitch Watson,
Emily Brundige, and Eric Shaw

Andrews McMeel
PUBLISHING®

Andrews McMeel Publishing
a division of Andrews McMeel Universal
1130 Walnut Street, Kansas City, Missouri 64106

www.andrewsmcmeel.com

Book design, layout, and lettering by The Story Division
www.thestorydivision.com

Editor: Lucas Wetzel
Art Director and Cover Design: Spencer Williams
Designer: Niko Dalcin
Production Editor: Dave Shaw
Copy Editor: Amy Strassner
Production Manager: Chuck Harper

Special thanks to:
Jeff Whitman, Jarrin Jacobs, Nathan Schram, and Flora Liang at Nickelodeon
Steffie Davis, Steve Osgoode, and Niko Dalcin at The Story Division
And special thanks to Lincoln Peirce for editorial guidance throughout this project.

22 23 24 25 26 SDB 10 9 8 7 6 5 4 3 2 1

ISBN (paperback): 978-1-5248-7873-3
ISBN (hardcover): 978-1-5248-7941-9

Library of Congress Control Number: 2022941200

Made by:
King Yip (Dongguan) Printing & Packaging Factory Ltd.
Address and location of production:
Daning Administrative District, Humen Town
Dongguan Guangdong, China 523930
1st Printing — 8/15/22

CONTENTS

How to Pull a Proper Prank

HEY GUYS, NATE WRIGHT HERE! PART OF BEING AWESOME IS KEEPING THE FANS HAPPY.
AND WHAT DO MY FANS LIKE MOST? PRANKS!
PRANK #1
E A R T H =
TODAY WE'LL BE LEARNING ABOUT CLIMATE CHANGE.
MY MOM SAYS CLIMATE CHANGE IS THE HOAX INVENTED TO DISMANTLE CAPITALISM!
UGH!

>SIGH.< WELL, IT'S REAL. I'LL PROVE IT TO YOU!
"LET'S HIT PAUSE FOR A SECOND..."
WHAT MR. GALVIN DOESN'T KNOW IS THAT I SLIPPED A BURRITO IN HIS POCKET...
...AND HID CHAD IN THE CABINET...
...DRESSED AS A RAT!

CHAD WILL DO ANYTHING FOR A BURRITO! SO WHEN HE SMELLS IT ON GALVIN...?
LET'S WATCH!
GRRRRR!
SNIFF!
SNIFF!

!
BURRITO!
AHHHHHH!
ONE OF THE LAB RATS MUST HAVE GOTTEN INTO MY GROWTH SERUM!
SPROING!

AHHHH!!

ARGHHHH!
AHHHH!!
SHLURRRP!

WAHHH!
EEEEK!
SHLURP!

EVER SINCE GINA—MY **NEMESIS** AND ALL-AROUND KISS-UP—SAW A VLOG ABOUT HOW YOU SHOULD DRINK WATER TO FIGHT ACNE, SHE'S BEEN DEEPLY PASSIONATE ABOUT HYDRATION!
LET'S HAVE SOME FUN, SHALL WE?
PRANK #2
WHICH ONE OF YOU LITTLE ***TOAST-HEADS*** CAN TELL ME WHEN THE DECLARATION OF INDEPENDENCE WAS SIGNED?
ANYONE?

ME! ME!
I KNOW THE ANSWER, MRS. GODFREY!
AUGUST 2ND, 1776!
CORRECT AGAIN, STAR PUPIL!
GROAN!

SWIPE!
KLINK!
GLUG!
GLUG!
GLUG!

GAG!
RIBBIT!
AHHHHHH! THEY'RE LICKING MY EYEBALLS!
CROOOAAKKK!

SOME OF MY GLOBAL FANBASE HAS ASKED IF I'VE EVER PRANKED MY FRIENDS? WELL, YES! IT'S BASICALLY MY SIGNATURE MOVE!
PRANK #3
AHHHHH!
BOINGGG!
CRASHHH!
OOOF!
DING!

PRANK #4
GRUNT!
YOU GUYS WANNA TRY SOMETHING REALLY TOUGH? YOU SHOULD DO ATOMIC SIT-UPS!
LIE BACK, CLOSE YOUR EYES, THEN TRY TO DO A SIT-UP.
YOU'LL SEE. IT'S STUPID HARD.

HUH?!
AHAHAHAHAHAHA!
HA
HA
HA
HA
HA
HA
DING!

ALWAYS REMEMBER, IF YOU DISH IT OUT, YOU GOTTA BE WILLING TO TAKE IT!
PRANK #5
OH HO!
HEH HEH HEH!
SQUISH!

HMM?
BLOOOP!
AHHHHHHHH!
POP!
GAME RESPECTS GAME.

AN OFT FORGOTTEN PRANKING **GOLD MINE** IS THE FAMILY HOME!
PRANK #6
BRUSH BRUSH BRUSH!
PTOO!
HUH?!

AHHHHHH!
HAHAHA!

CLICK!
NATE!!!
I THINK IT'S AN IMPROVEMENT!

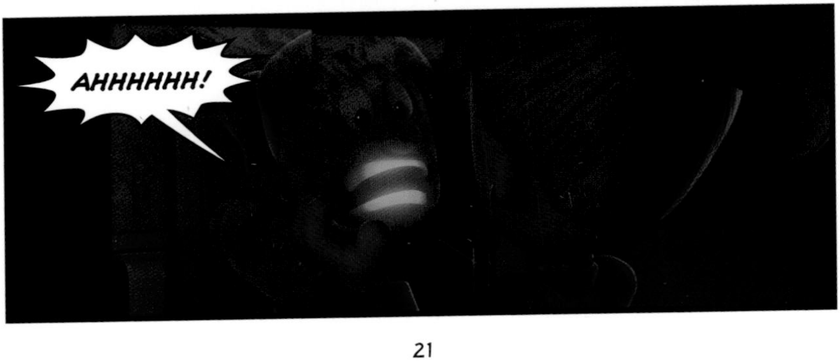
AHHHHHH!

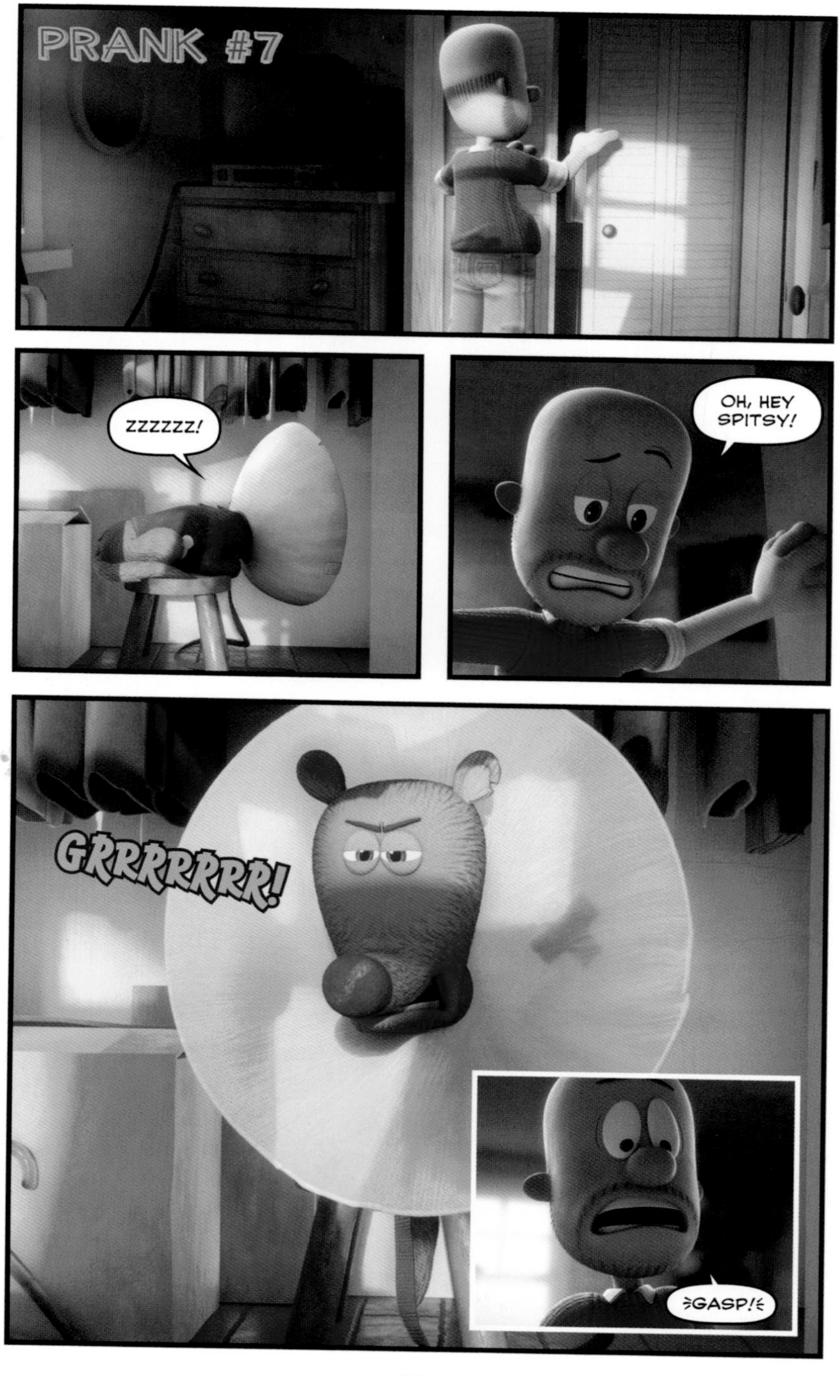
PRANK #7
ZZZZZZ!
OH, HEY SPITSY!
GRRRRRRR!
GASP!

AHHHHHH!
GRR!
CRASH!

WHEN IT COMES TO PRANKS, YOU JUST GOTTA LET YOUR CREATIVE JUICES FLOW! YOU GOTTA **OWN IT.** BE YOU. **BE AWESOME!**
IS THAT **MY** PHONE?!
UH-OH!
CRASH!

DAD!
OWW, MY ELBOW!
GIVE IT BACK!
OW! DAD, ELLEN HIT ME!
UH, CAN SOMEONE PLEASE HELP ME GET THE NEIGHBOR'S DOG OFF MY BUTT?!
DING!

COMPOSITION
NATE FILES
WIDE RULE
The Pimple

Chapter 1
THIS IS BAD!

ZZZZZ...
CHIP

YAWNNN!
CHIP

AHHHHH!
CHIP
THUD!

YAWN!
HUH?
AAHHHHH!

OH, THIS IS **BAD!** THIS IS LIKE WORLD WAR III WRAPPED UP IN A ZOMBIE APOCALYPSE **BAD!**
HEY, DORK, GET OUT OF THE BATHROOM! *GASP!* WHA-WH-WH-**WHAT?!**
OH, **MAN!** AND YOU CALL **ME** THE ZIT QUEEN! **AHAHAHAHAHA!**
SHUT YOUR PIPE, ELLEN!
I HAVE THIS TOTALLY UNDER CONTROL!
WHAT DO I DO?! IF I SHOW UP TO SCHOOL WITH THIS THING, I'M GONNA BE **SHAMED!**
"**MOCKED!**
HAHA!
HA
HA HA
HAHA!
"**LAUGHED AT!**
HAHA!
HA
HA
HAHAHA!
HAHAHA!

EARTH=
"OH, HOW THEY'LL LAUGH!"
HAHA
HA
HAHA!
HAHA
HAHAHA!
THERE'S ONLY *ONE THING* FOR ME TO DO...
SQUEEZE!
WHOA, WHOA, *WHOA!*
POPPING IT IS ONLY GOING TO MAKE IT A *MILLION TIMES* WORSE! I SHOULD KNOW, I *AM* THE ZIT QUEEN!
A *MILLION* TIMES WORSE? WHAT DID OLD CACKLE PANTS MEAN BY *THAT?!*

"WILL MY PIMPLE SEEK *REVENGE?*
AHHHH!
ROOAAAR!
"WILL IT BECOME AN *UNSTOPPABLE MEGA PIMPLE BLOB?!*

AHHHH!
ROOAAAR!
"WILL IT MEAN... THE END?!"
SOB!
NATE
WAHHHHH! HE WAS SO YOUNG!
YOU KNOW WHAT? I THINK I BETTER TRUST ELLEN ON THIS ONE. AFTER ALL, SHE IS THE ZIT QUEEN.
AND HEY... MAYBE NO ONE WILL NOTICE!
ZIP!

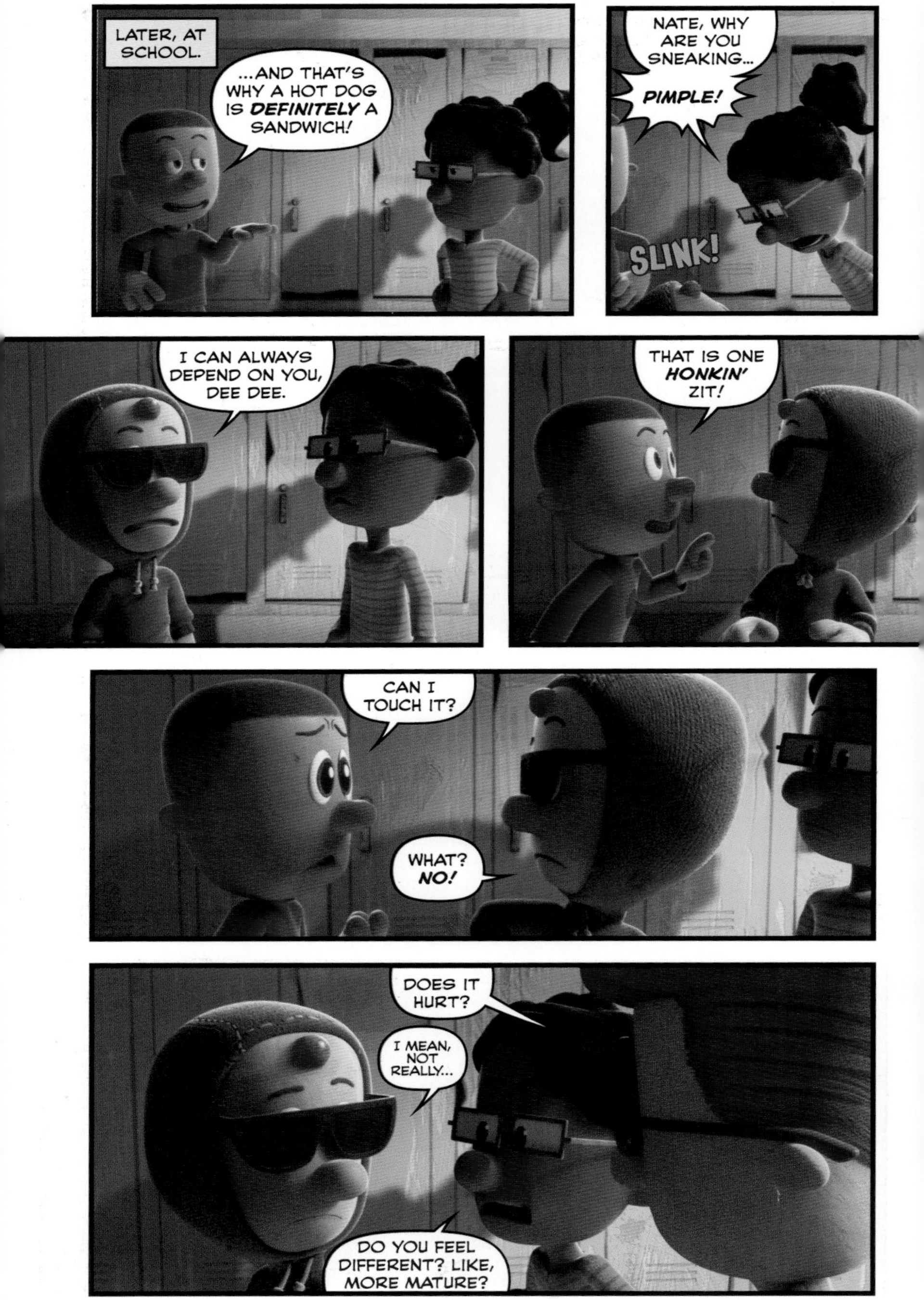

LATER, AT SCHOOL.
...AND THAT'S WHY A HOT DOG IS DEFINITELY A SANDWICH!
NATE, WHY ARE YOU SNEAKING...
PIMPLE!
SLINK!
I CAN ALWAYS DEPEND ON YOU, DEE DEE.
THAT IS ONE HONKIN' ZIT!
CAN I TOUCH IT?
WHAT? NO!
DOES IT HURT?
I MEAN, NOT REALLY...
DO YOU FEEL DIFFERENT? LIKE, MORE MATURE?

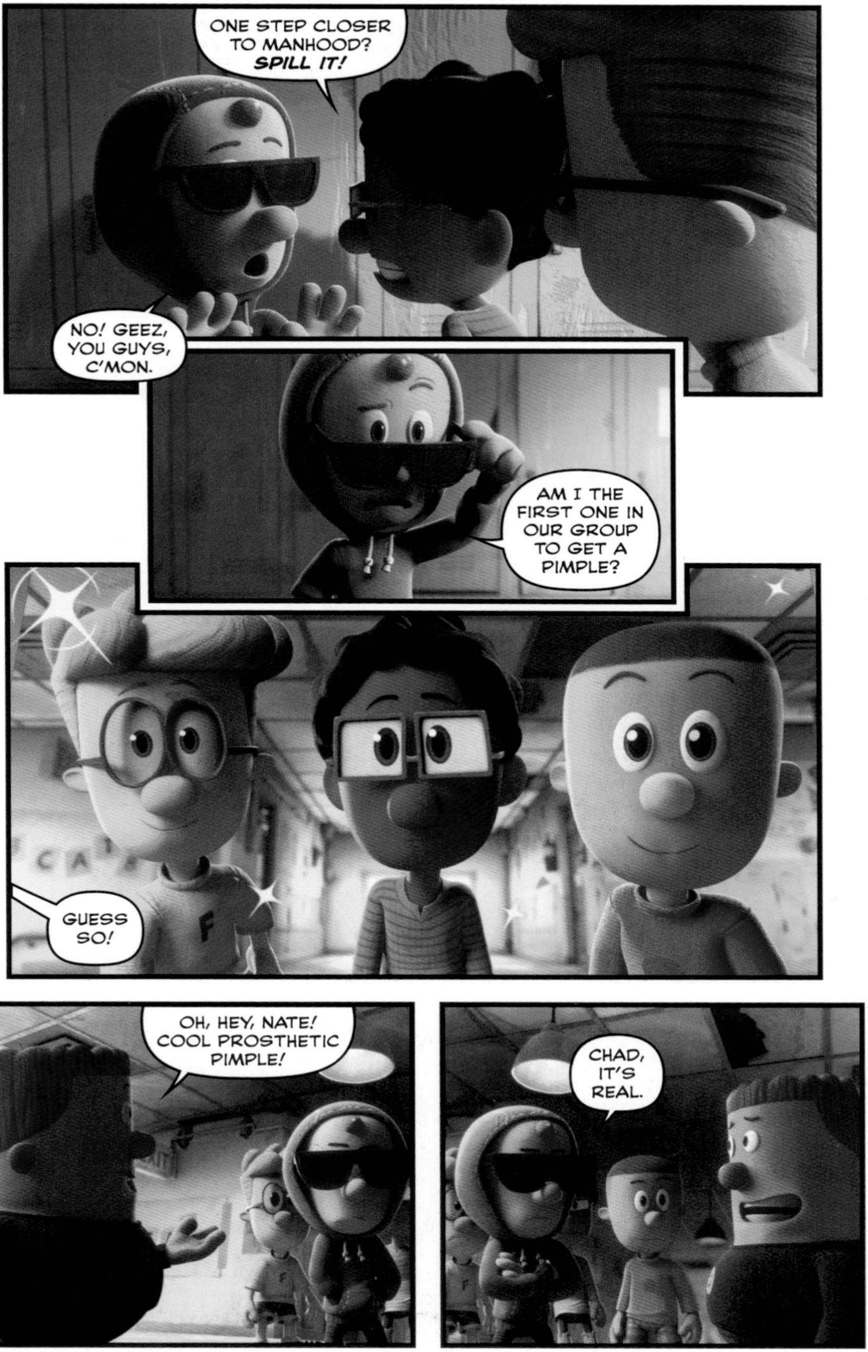
ONE STEP CLOSER TO MANHOOD? SPILL IT!
NO! GEEZ, YOU GUYS, C'MON.
AM I THE FIRST ONE IN OUR GROUP TO GET A PIMPLE?
GUESS SO!
OH, HEY, NATE! COOL PROSTHETIC PIMPLE!
CHAD, IT'S REAL.

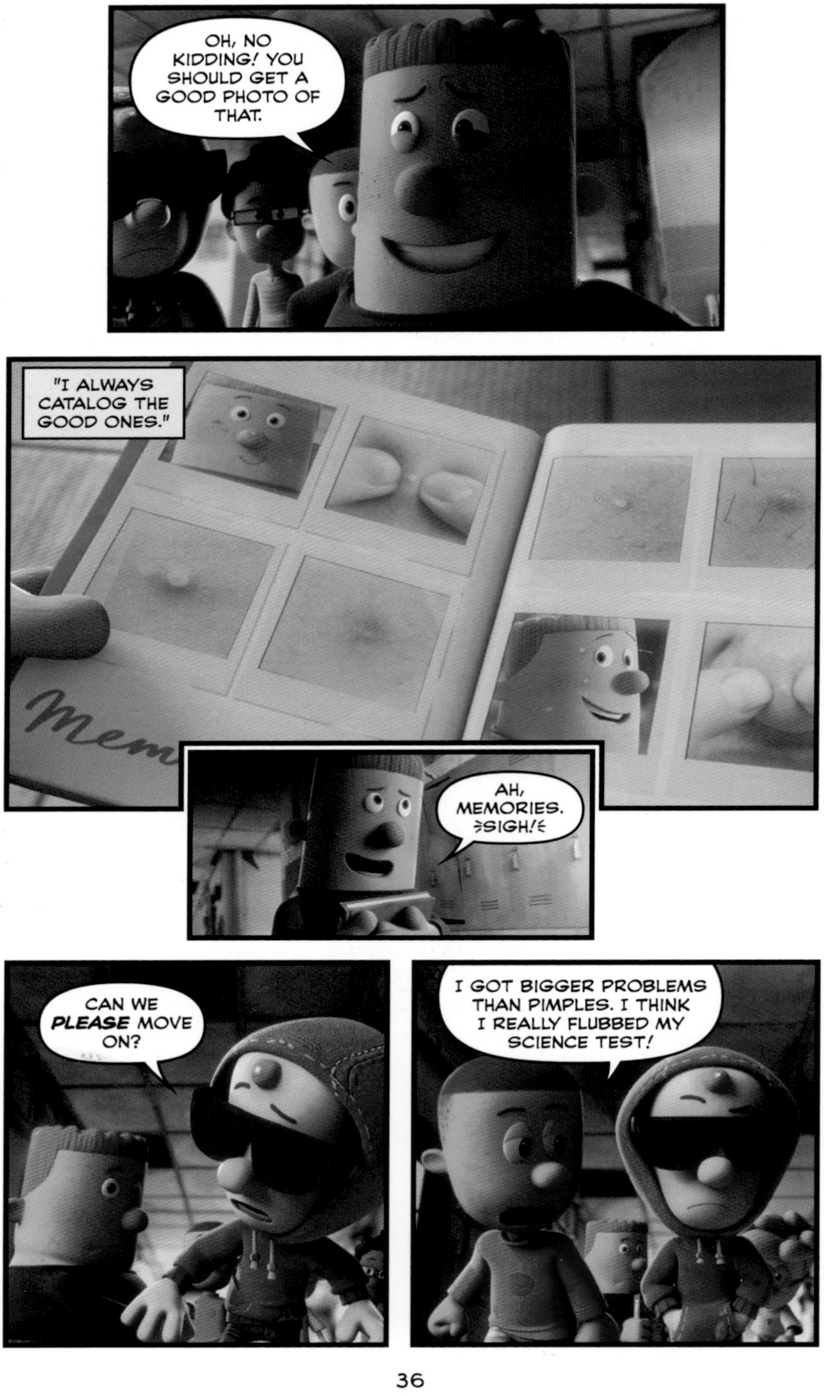
OH, NO KIDDING! YOU SHOULD GET A GOOD PHOTO OF THAT.
"I ALWAYS CATALOG THE GOOD ONES."
Mem
AH, MEMORIES. SIGH!
CAN WE *PLEASE* MOVE ON?
I GOT BIGGER PROBLEMS THAN PIMPLES. I THINK I REALLY FLUBBED MY SCIENCE TEST!

WHAT HAPPENED? I THOUGHT YOU STUDIED!

WELL, YEAH, I WAS GOING TO STUDY, BUT I HAD TO HELP UNCLE PEDRO TRAIN FERRETS FOR HIS RODENT CIRCUS!
DIDN'T HAVE THE HEART TO TELL HIM FERRETS AREN'T RODENTS.

YOU KNOW WHO IS A RODENT? MY DRAMA TEACHER, DR. LAGAZE!

HE KEEPS CASTING ME IN SMALLER AND SMALLER ROLES. THIS SEMESTER, I'M PLAYING THE ROLE OF THE SEAWEED IN "DEATH OF A SAILORMAN."

THE ***SEAWEED!*** TALK ABOUT TALENT ***WASTED!***

JUST LEMME TOUCH IT!

OOOOOH! PLEASE, NATE...
I'VE BEEN FASCINATED WITH PIMPLES SINCE I WAS A BABY!
SHOVE!

YOU'RE GONNA DRAW MORE ATTENTION TO IT!
MIGHTY FINE PIMPLE THERE, NATE!

AWWWW! NATE-NATE'S GOT A PIMPIE! HAHAHA!
AH! AHHH!
AHHHH!!!!
GOTCHA!
DOINK!
BOING!
BOING!
BOING!
I FEEL PERSONALLY VIOLATED.

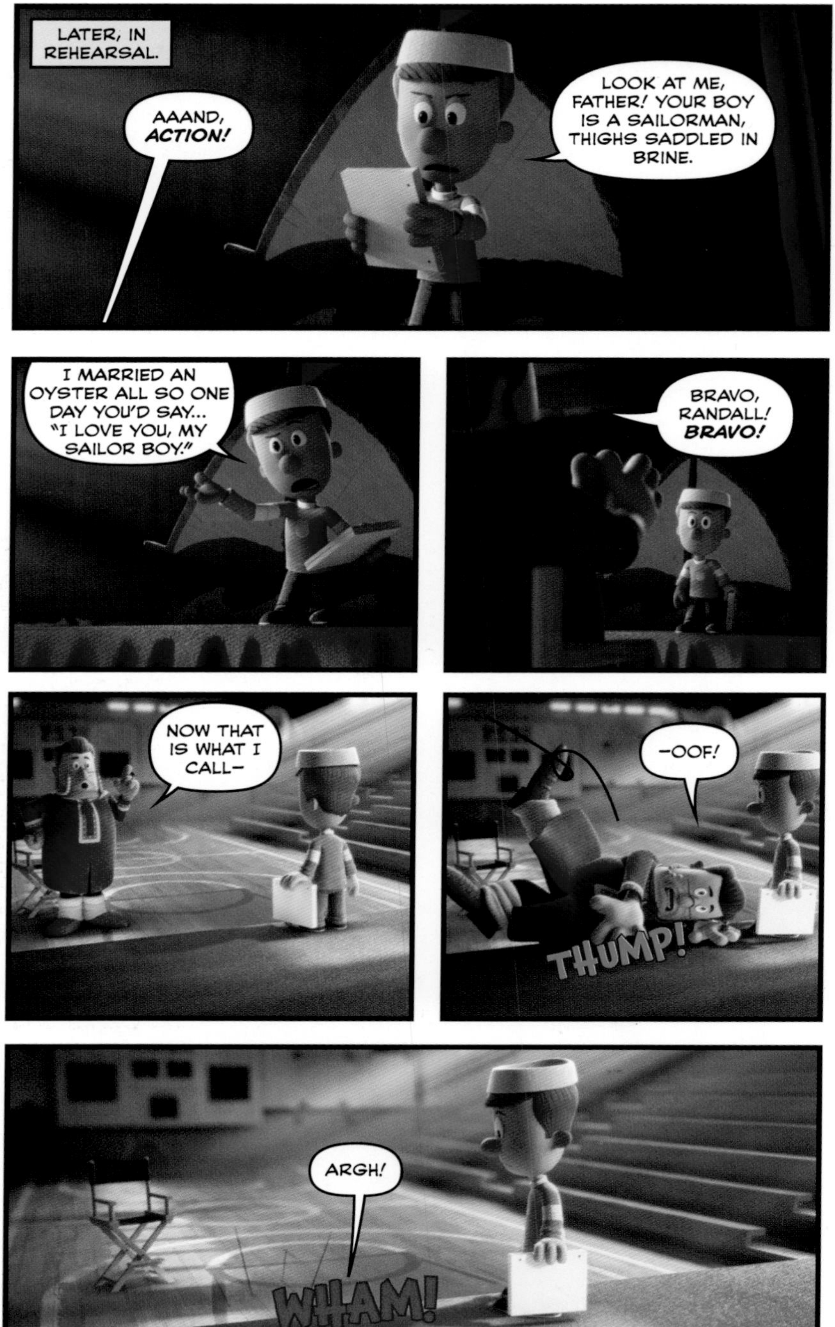
LATER, IN REHEARSAL.
AAAND, ACTION!
LOOK AT ME, FATHER! YOUR BOY IS A SAILORMAN, THIGHS SADDLED IN BRINE.
I MARRIED AN OYSTER ALL SO ONE DAY YOU'D SAY... "I LOVE YOU, MY SAILOR BOY."
BRAVO, RANDALL! BRAVO!
NOW THAT IS WHAT I CALL—
—OOF!
THUMP!
ARGH!
WHAM!

FLIP!
-ACTING!
BUT HE WASN'T SHOWING ***ANY*** EMOTION!
EMOTIONS ARE FOR BABIES AND POETS. WE ARE ***ACTORS!***
ALL WE HAVE TO REMEMBER IS OUR ***DRAMATIC PRODUCE***.
OBSERVE.

THE ONION!
FSSSSP!
SOB!
OH, TRAGEDY! MY DOG HAS RUN AWAY!
THE BANANA!
OH, JOY! MY DOG HAS RETURNED!

THE TOMATO!
OH, AGONY!
SPLAT!
HE'S JUST BITTEN MY LEG.
MMM, THE FLAVOR!
AS LIFE IMITATES ART, SO TOO SHALL I HAVE TOMATO SOUP FOR LUNCH!
HI! MR. LAGAZE?

PLEASE! I HAVE A DOCTORATE IN DRAMATIC PRODUCE!
SORRY. DOCTOR... LAGAZE.
I HAD SOME QUESTIONS ABOUT MY CHARACTER, THE SEAWEED?
GO ON. I'M SORT OF LISTENING.
WHAT'S HER BACKSTORY?
IS SHE AWARE OF OCEAN ACIDIFICATION AND THE HAVOC IT'S PLAYING ON CORAL REEFS?
AND HOW DOES SHE FEEL ABOUT THE SAILORMAN?

YOU'RE A **SEAWEED,** DEE DEE. YOU'RE SLIMY AND GREEN AND **NOBODY LIKES YOU.**

OH, AND YOU GO LIKE THIS...
OOOLAA GOOLA GOOLA!

GROAN!

LUNCHTIME.
I'M NOT REALLY SURE WHAT I'M EATING...BUT I THINK MAYBE IT'S A...BEAN?
IZZIT?
OOP! I SAID "ZIT," DIDN'T I? SORRY, NATE, I DIDN'T MEAN TO CALL ATTENTION TO YOUR GINORMOUS PIMPLE.
THAT'S OKAY, CHAD.
HERE, NATE, TRY SOME BEANS, I INSIST!
UH...NO, NOT "CYST"! I WAS TRYING TO SAY...

...HELP ME OUT, DEE DEE! WHAT WAS I TRYING TO SAY?
BLACKHEAD.
NO!
PUSTULE.
I GIVE UP!
SIGH.
WELL, ACCORDING TO DR. LAGAZE, I HAVE NOTHING TO SAY, SO I DON'T EVEN KNOW WHY YOU ASKED ME.
SIGH.
GUYS, GUYS, GUYS! IT'S A DANG MIRACLE!

I GOT AN "A" ON MY SCIENCE TEST! ALL BECAUSE I TOUCHED YOUR ZIT!

YOU'VE GOT A ***LUCKY PIMPLE,*** MAN!

C'MON, TEDDY. THAT'S RIDICULOUS! A PIMPLE CAN'T BE LUCKY!

LET ME TRY. COME ON, LADY LUCK!

BOOP!

SEE? I'M STILL A SEA–
SILENCE! I HAVE AN ANNOUNCEMENT TO MAKE! I'M TAKING A LEAVE OF ABSENCE.
HOLLYWOOD CALLED. I GOT A SMASHING ROLE IN A HIT SCIENCE FICTION MOVIE FRANCHISE!
GROAN!
SPLAT!
I'M SO HAPPY I COULD CRY...
SPRITZ!
...OH, THE PAIN!

FAREWELL, MY FORMER STUDENTS AND ***LESS TALENTED*** COLLEAGUES! GOOD LUCK WITH THE REST OF YOUR HUMDRUM LIVES.
I'M CATCHING THE GLORY TRAIN TO LEGENDVILLE!
OOF!
THUMP!
I'M FINE. JUST A LITTLE ONION BLINDNESS.

IS IT A MERE COINCIDENCE THAT DEE DEE TOUCHED MY PIMPLE AND NOW HER BLOWHARD DRAMA TEACHER'S GOING AWAY?
I THINK **NOT!** SOONER OR LATER, AWESOMENESS **ALWAYS** HITS ITS MARK!
GANG, ME AND THIS LUCKY PIMPLE ARE GOING TO CHANGE THE WORLD!

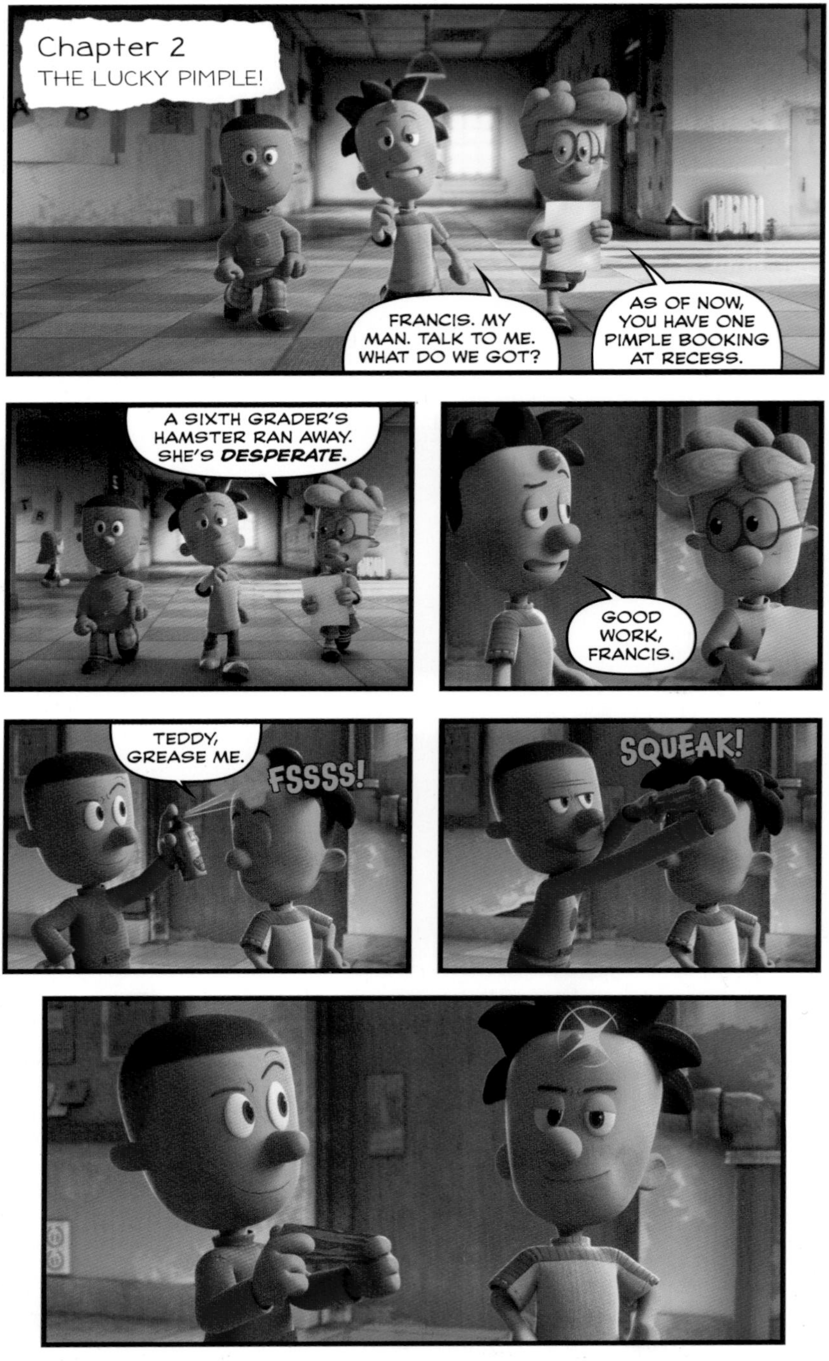
Chapter 2
THE LUCKY PIMPLE!
FRANCIS. MY MAN. TALK TO ME. WHAT DO WE GOT?
AS OF NOW, YOU HAVE ONE PIMPLE BOOKING AT RECESS.
A SIXTH GRADER'S HAMSTER RAN AWAY. SHE'S *DESPERATE*.
GOOD WORK, FRANCIS.
TEDDY, GREASE ME.
FSSSS!
SQUEAK!

ALL RIGHT, DEE DEE, HOW'S THE DRAMA OUTREACH GOING?
I'M ON IT.
THAT'S WHAT I LIKE TO HEAR.
MM-HMM!
ALL RIGHT, LET'S GO OUT THERE AND SPREAD THE GOOD WORD!

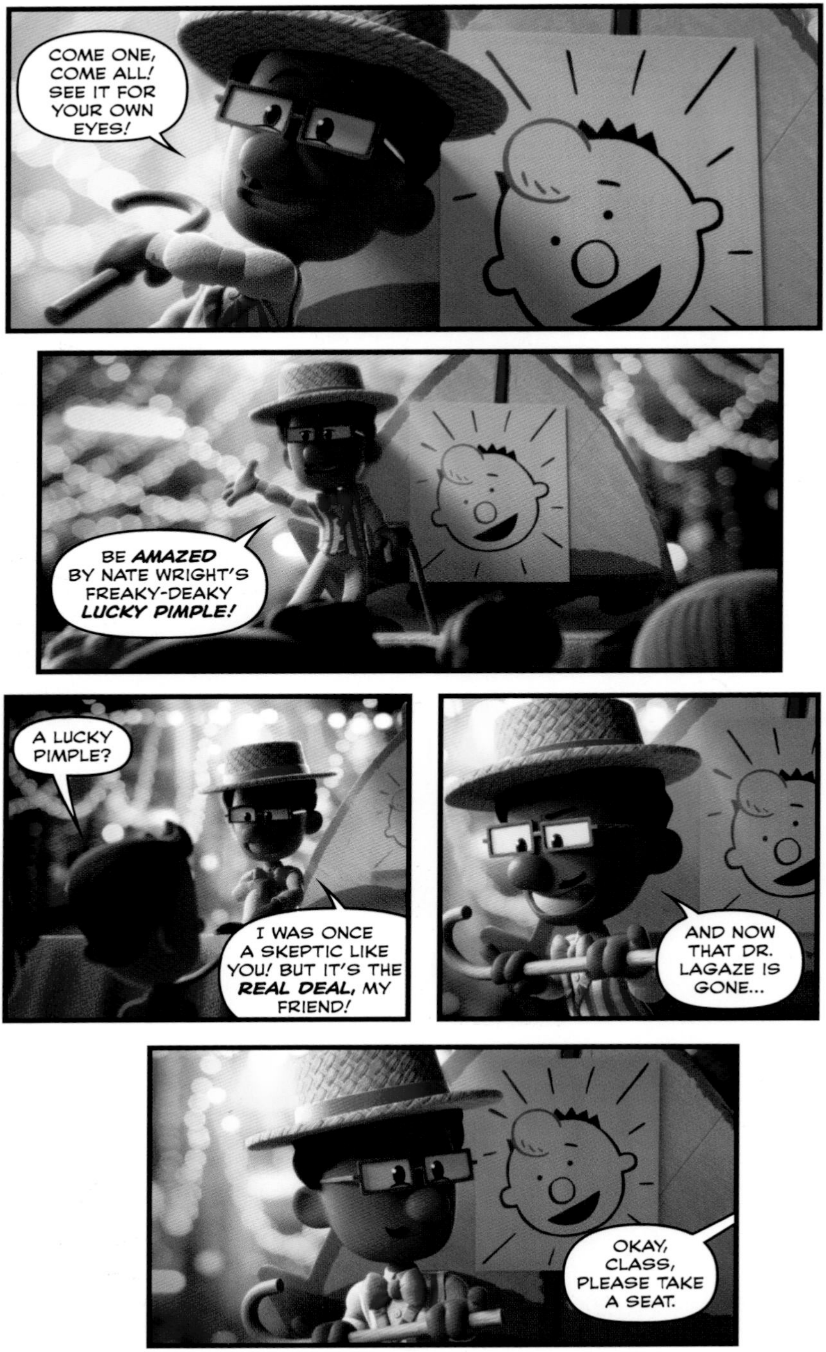
COME ONE, COME ALL! SEE IT FOR YOUR OWN EYES!
BE AMAZED BY NATE WRIGHT'S FREAKY-DEAKY LUCKY PIMPLE!
A LUCKY PIMPLE?
I WAS ONCE A SKEPTIC LIKE YOU! BUT IT'S THE REAL DEAL, MY FRIEND!
AND NOW THAT DR. LAGAZE IS GONE...
OKAY, CLASS, PLEASE TAKE A SEAT.

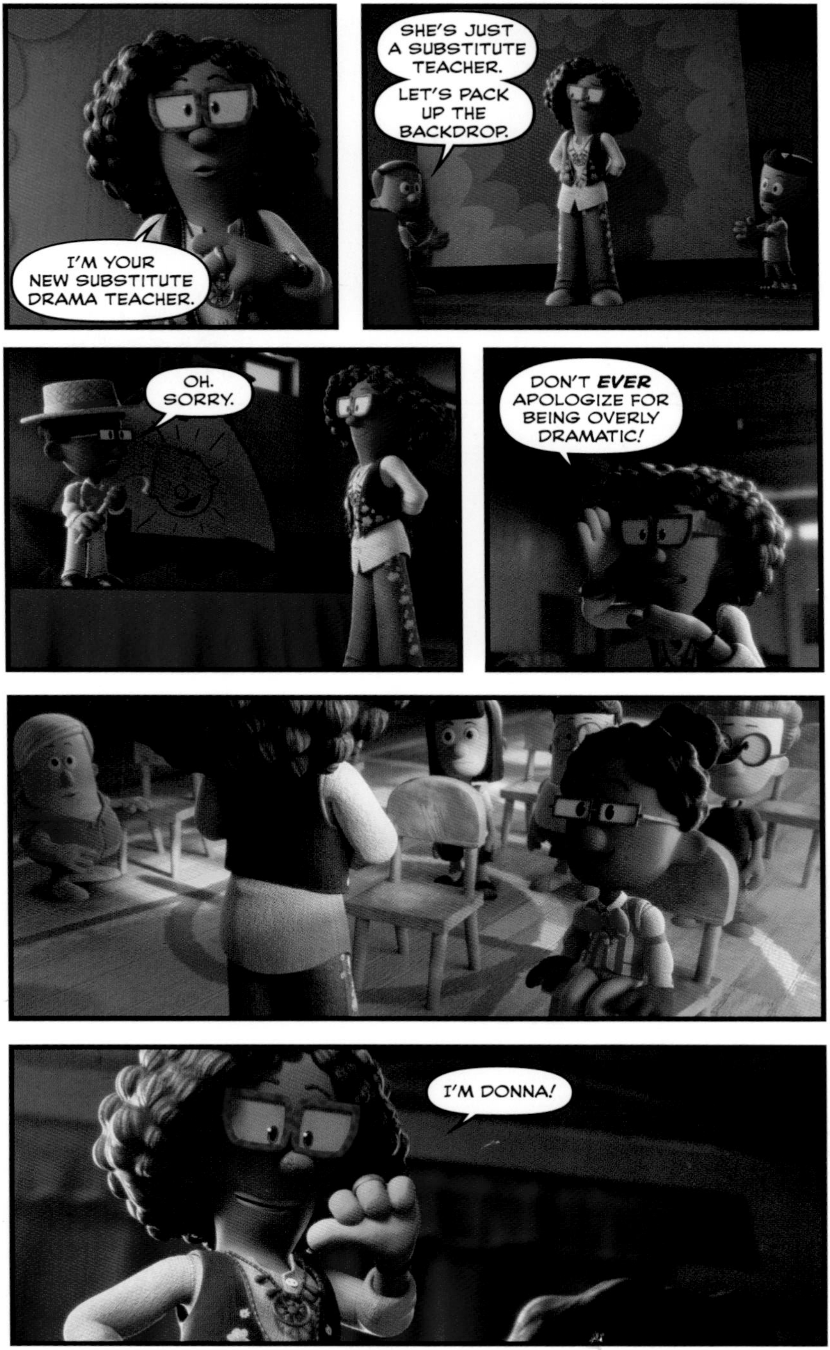
I'M YOUR NEW SUBSTITUTE DRAMA TEACHER.
SHE'S JUST A SUBSTITUTE TEACHER.
LET'S PACK UP THE BACKDROP.
OH. SORRY.
DON'T ***EVER*** APOLOGIZE FOR BEING OVERLY DRAMATIC!
I'M DONNA!

FWIP!
"D" STANDS FOR DRAMA.
"O" STANDS FOR OBSESSION.

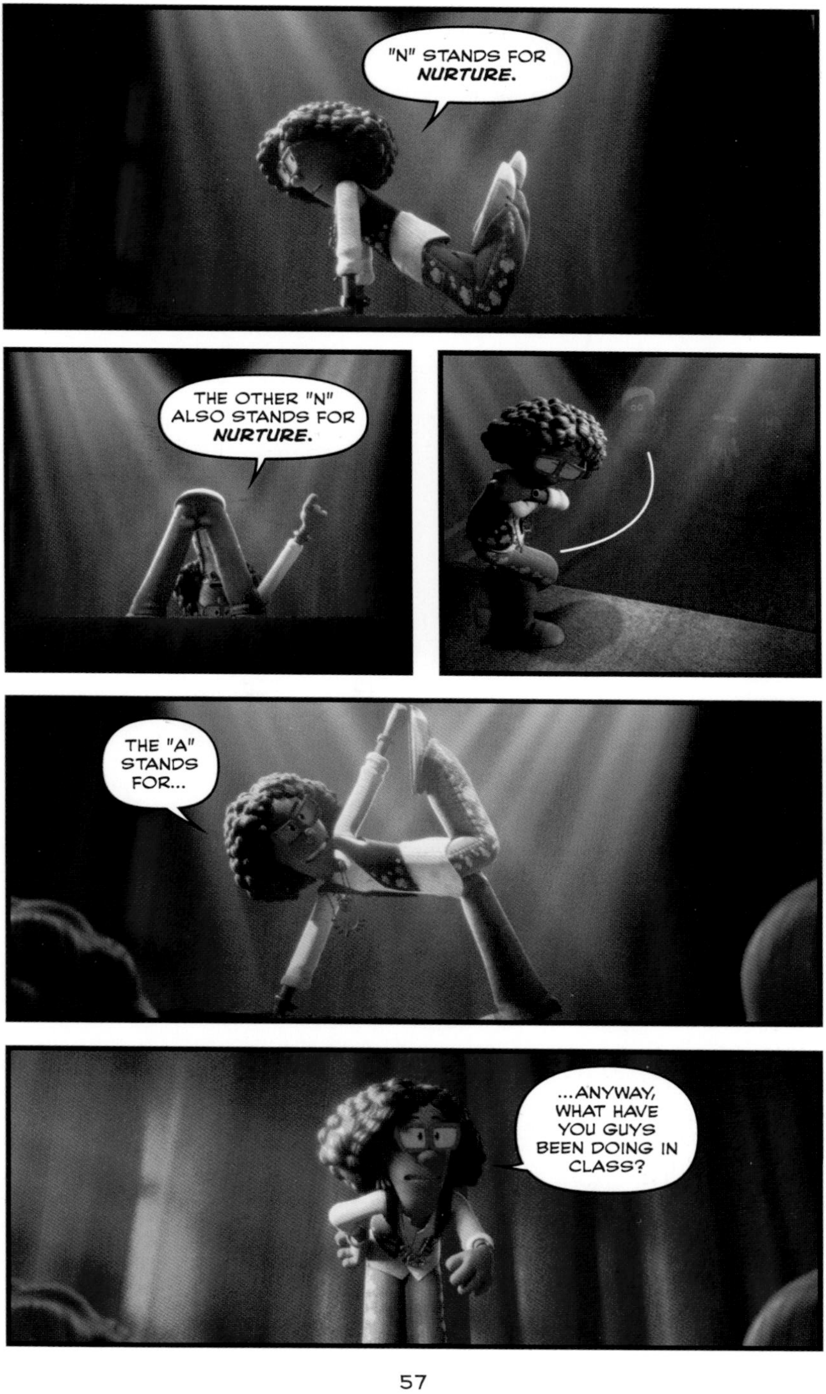
"N" STANDS FOR NURTURE.
THE OTHER "N" ALSO STANDS FOR NURTURE.
THE "A" STANDS FOR...
...ANYWAY, WHAT HAVE YOU GUYS BEEN DOING IN CLASS?

WE'RE SUPPOSED TO BE REHEARSING FOR "DEATH OF A SAILORMAN."
YOU MEAN "SALESMAN"?
NO. IT'S A PLAY OUR OLD DRAMA TEACHER WROTE.
REALLY. CAN I SEE THE SCRIPT?

RRRRRIP!
OHHH!
HUH?
I'M SURE WHATEVER'S HAPPENING IN YOUR OWN LIVES IS MUCH MORE INTERESTING THAN WHAT'S IN THAT SCRIPT.
I LEARNED THAT WHEN I DID MY ONE-WOMAN PLAY, "THE DONNALOGUES," ON BROADWAY.
YOU WERE ON BROADWAY?!

YES, BUT I LEFT IT ALL BEHIND TO PURSUE MY **REAL** PASSION.
BEING A ***SUBSTITUTE DRAMA TEACHER!***
NOW, I WANT TO HEAR FROM YOU ALL.
TELL ME SOMETHING THAT HAPPENED YESTERDAY THAT ***MOVED*** YOU.
I CRUSHED A BUG.
AND HOW DID THAT MAKE YOU FEEL?
POWERFUL.
OKAY. THANK YOU...?

RANDY. OR RAD-SAUCE. OR RANDMAN.
OF COURSE... ANYONE ELSE?
MY FORMER DRAMA TEACHER TOLD ME THAT I WAS SLIMY AND GREEN AND THAT **NOBODY LIKED ME.**
AND HOW DID THAT MAKE YOU FEEL?
LIKE THE BUG THAT RANDY—
RAD-SAUCE.
...THAT RAD-SAUCE CRUSHED. I FELT STEPPED ON. IT MADE ME WANT TO **SCREAM!**

SO, WHY DON'T YOU?
AAAAHHHHHHHHHHHHH
AAHHHHHHHHHHHHHH!
BOOM!
BOOM!
CRACK!
CRACK!

THANK YOU... UM?
DEE DEE. THE NAME'S DEE DEE.
CLASS, I WANT YOU ALL TO RECOGNIZE DEE DEE'S ***BRAVERY*** HERE TODAY.
WOW!

AFTER CLASS.
HUH?
NATE!
NATE! YOU'LL NEVER BELIEVE IT!
THE NEW DRAMA TEACHER'S AMAZING SHE DID THIS DANCE AND HAD A SHOW ON BROADWAY AND SHE THINKS–
WHOA, WHOA. OKAY, DEE DEE, SLOW IT DOWN.
...THINKSSSS... I'MMMMMMMM... BRAAAAAAAAAVE...

YOU KNOW, IN HINDSIGHT, I SHOULD HAVE BEEN MUCH MORE SPECIFIC ABOUT MY INSTRUCTIONS.
NATE WRIGHT!
THAT'S ME.
WHAM!

I TOUCHED YOUR PIMPLE THIS MORNING, AND MR. SQUIGGLES CAME BACK TO ME!
DID YOU HEAR THAT?
NATE WRIGHT'S PIMPLE BROUGHT MY HAMSTER BACK!
WELL WHAT DO YOU HAVE TO SAY FOR YOURSELF, NATE WRIGHT?
UH...BLESSED BE THE PIMPLE?

SQUEAK!
BLESSED BE THE PIMPLE!
BLESSED BE NATE WRIGHT!
BLESSED BE THE PIMPLE!
BLESSED BE NATE WRIGHT!

LATER.
STEP UPPETH AND RECEIVE THE PROMISE OF THE PIMPLE!
I TRIED TO CUT MY OWN HAIR AND THIS IS WHAT HAPPENED! NOW I'LL NEVER GET A GIRLFRIEND!
THAT'S FOR THE PIMPLE TO DECIDE!
BOOP!

OH, UH, HEY TRENDSETTER! HOT HAIRCUT! WANNA CUT MY HAIR LATER?
!!!
NATE, MY LEG IS BUSTED AND THE CHAMPIONSHIP GAME IS NEXT WEEK!
AH, YES, THE GREAT PIMPLE HAS HEARD YOU!
BOOP!

BY THE POWER OF THE PIMPLE, I SHALL BECOME THE ULTIMATE SOCCER PLAYER!
HI-YA!
CRSSSH!
HEADS UP!
FWOOSH!
BLAM!
WHAM!
OOF!
ALL GOOD!

LATER.
GOTTA KEEP THIS PIMPLE FED!
SPLOOSH
RUB!
RUB!
RUB!
SLURP!
GASP!

THE PRINCIPAL'S OFFICE.
NATE, HERE'S THE BOTTOM LINE...
...I GOT A TIP ON SOME MONKEY-POWERED WINDMILLS, AND... WELL...
OO-OO! AH-AH!
SCREECH!
"IT WAS NOT A GOOD INVESTMENT."
FWOOSH!

I'M BROKE! I JUST NEED ONE BIG SCORE TO GET ME BACK ON MY FEET!
LET ME TOUCH YOUR PIMPLE, AND I PROMISE YOU'LL NEVER HAVE TO GO TO DETENTION FOR THE REST OF YOUR LIFE!
BOOP!

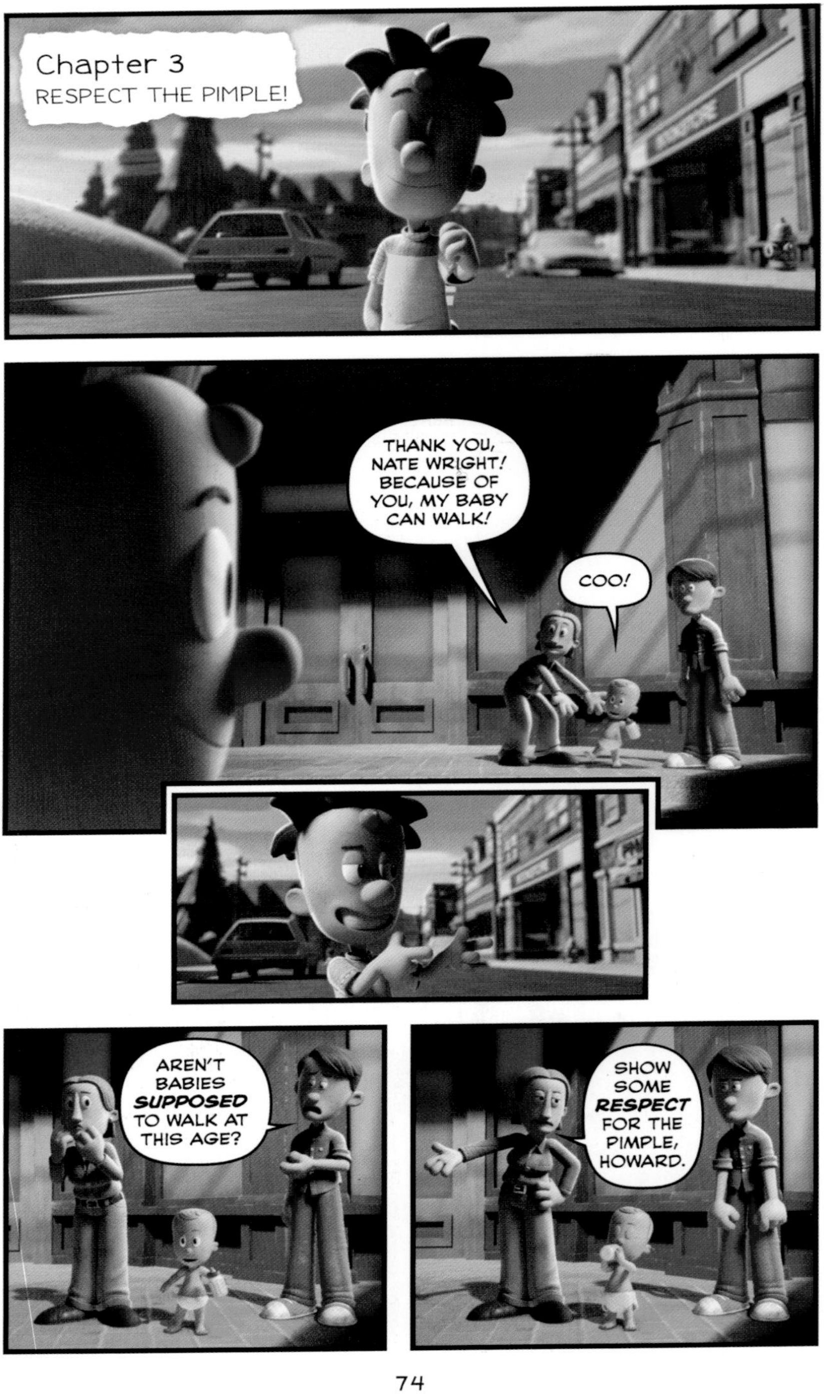

Chapter 3
RESPECT THE PIMPLE!
THANK YOU, NATE WRIGHT! BECAUSE OF YOU, MY BABY CAN WALK!
COO!
AREN'T BABIES SUPPOSED TO WALK AT THIS AGE?
SHOW SOME RESPECT FOR THE PIMPLE, HOWARD.

PIMPLE MERCH, PIMPLE MERCH HERE! GET IT BEFORE IT ***POPS!***
FSHHHHH!
WHY ISN'T THIS ZIT WORKING?!
YOU CAN'T ***FORCE*** AWESOMENESS, FELLAS.

MEANWHILE, IN REHEARSAL...
IT WAS THE SUMMER OF MY SIXTH YEAR. I REMEMBER THE SMELL OF HYDRANGEAS.

MY PARENTS WERE HAVING A YARD SALE AND I WAS ASKED TO GET RID OF SOME OF MY STUFFED ANIMALS.

A CHILD SHOULD ***NEVER*** HAVE TO MAKE SUCH A CHOICE!

I TRIED TO TAKE IT BACK, BUT IT WAS TOO LATE. CHARLIE THE PENGUIN WAS GONE! AND I WAS LEFT WITH AN EMPTY SPACE ON MY COMFORTER!

CLAP
CLAP
CLAP
CLAP
CLAP
HONK!
DEE DEE! HANG BACK A MINUTE.
I HAVE SOMETHING FOR YOU.

Uta Hagen
A Challenge for the Actor
WHAT'S THIS?
DEE DEE, I THINK YOU'VE GOT A REAL *GIFT.*
KEEP PRACTICING YOUR CRAFT AND YOU MIGHT JUST FIND THE ACTOR INSIDE THE ACTOR INSIDE THE PERSON INSIDE THE PERSON IN *YOU.*

LATER.
YA KNOW, I CAN EAT ALL THE GREASY FAST FOOD I WANT!
JUST MAKES THE PIMPLE MORE POWERFUL!
GIGGLE!
PTOOO!
NATE! WHAT ARE YOU DOING?
I'M JUST SPENDING SOME QUALITY TIME WITH MY FANS.
OH YEAH? WELL ARE THEY HERE FOR YOU, OR FOR YOUR PIMPLE?!

⪢COUGH!⪡ JEALOUS. ⪢COUGH!⪡ SO PAINFULLY JEALOUS. ⪢COUGH!⪡ SORRY, I HAD SOMETHING IN MY THROAT. I WAS SAYING YOU'RE JEALOUS.
GRRR!
DON'T LET THAT PIMPLE WRITE A CHECK YOUR BUTT CAN'T CASH!
BOOP!
EWW. REMOVE HER!
NOOO!

YOU CAN'T DO THIS TO ME!

I'M THE ZIT QUEEEEN!

SPLOORSH!

NOM NOM NOM!
SLURP!

THE NEXT DAY.
NOK! NOK!
DEE DEE! WHAT A LOVELY SURPRISE!
I FOUND YOUR ADDRESS IN THE SUBSTITUTE TEACHER PAGES.
OH, WHO IS YOUR LITTLE FRIEND, DONNA?

OH, HOW RUDE OF ME! THIS IS KATHLEEN, MY WIFE.
"WIFE"...?
HI, DEE DEE! DON, IS THIS THE *TALENTED YOUNG ACTRESS* YOU'VE BEEN TELLING ME ABOUT?

IT CERTAINLY IS.
WELL, UH, SORRY TO JUST SHOW UP AT YOUR HOUSE LIKE THIS, BUT I HAD SOME QUESTIONS ABOUT THIS BOOK.
AS *DEDICATED* AS I THOUGHT YOU WERE! COME IN, COME IN. I'LL MAKE SOME TEA.

MONDAY AT SCHOOL.
YOU'RE SO WISE, NATE. I CAN'T BELIEVE YOU'RE ONLY IN SIXTH GRADE!
Y'KNOW, YOU'RE NOT THE FIRST SEVENTH-GRADE GIRL TO TELL ME THAT THIS WEEK.

FLY AWAY, LITTLE BIRDIES!
HEY, JENNY!
WOULD YOU LIKE TO TOUCH MY PIMPLE?
GRR! HEY, GIVE ME A TOUCH!
GROSS!!!
EWWW!
NO, JENNY, WAIT!

YOU OKAY UP THERE BUDDY?
NATE!
HOW COULD YOU **DO** THIS TO ME?!
WHAT? WHAT ARE YOU TALKING ABOUT, TEDDY?
BECAUSE OF THE "A" I GOT ON MY SCIENCE TEST, I'M BEING SENT TO A GIFTED SUMMER SCHOOL FOR EXCEPTIONAL CHILDREN!
I'M NOT EXCEPTIONAL **OR** GIFTED!
WELL, NOW YOU'RE JUST STATING THE OBVIOUS...AND NONE OF THAT IS ***MY*** FAULT!

IT'S ALL YOUR FAULT! I SHOULD HAVE NEVER TOUCHED YOUR PIMPLE. THIS ISN'T MY HAMSTER AT ALL!
MY PARENTS LIED TO ME! IF THEY EVEN ARE MY PARENTS!
MY WHOLE LIFE HAS BEEN A LIE!!!
AHHHHH!
YOU! NATE WRIGHT! MY LEG WAS STILL BROKEN! NOW I'M GONNA HAVE TO WEAR THIS HUGE CAST UNTIL I'M FORTY!
AND THEN THEY'RE GONNA HAVE TO STRETCH MY LEG FOR ANOTHER TEN YEARS TO GET IT TO MATCH MY OTHER LEG!
MY SOCCER CAREER IS OVER!
GASP!
DO YOU KNOW HOW HARD IT IS TO MAINTAIN THIS BAD HAIRCUT? DO YOU?!

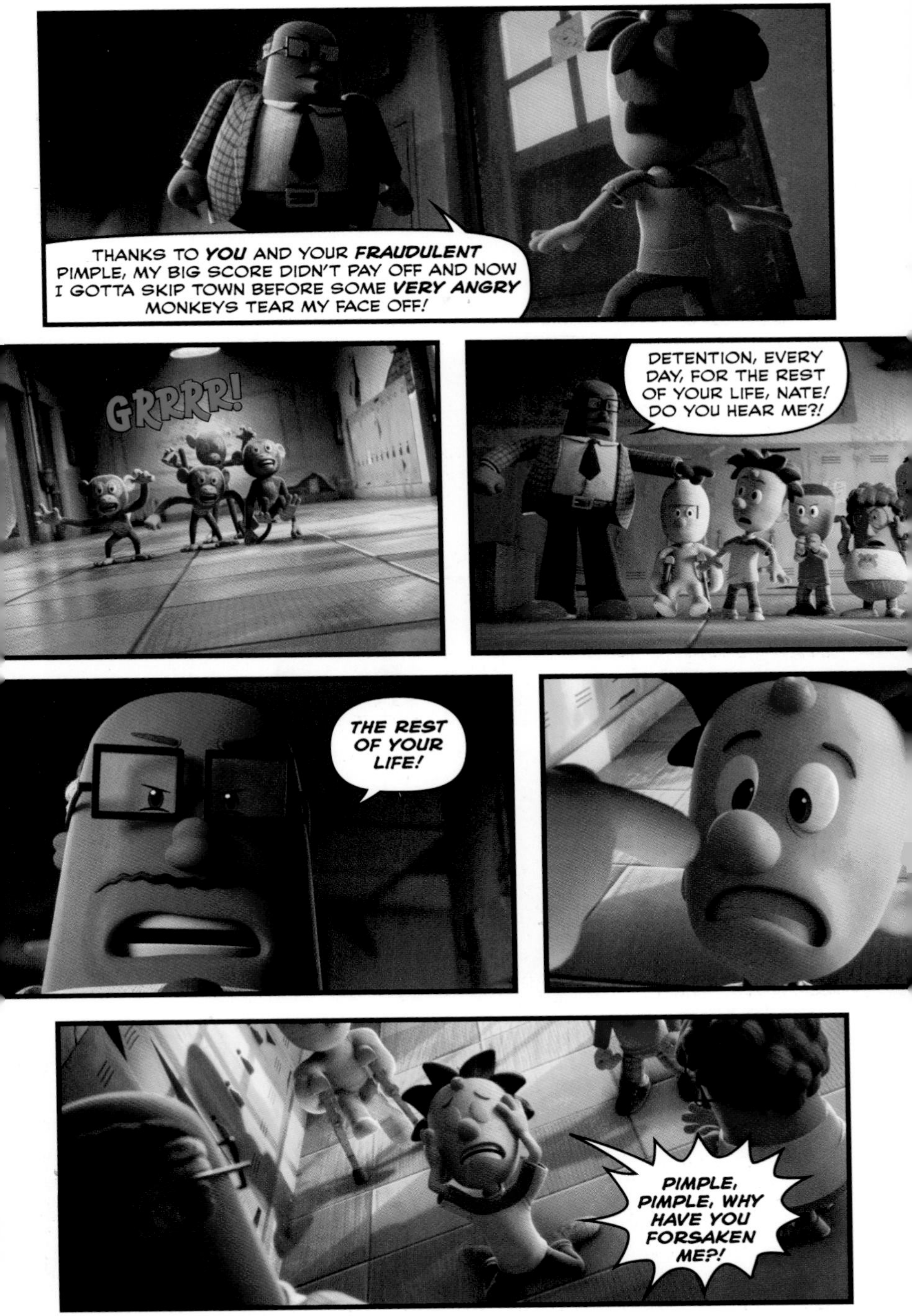
THANKS TO YOU AND YOUR FRAUDULENT PIMPLE, MY BIG SCORE DIDN'T PAY OFF AND NOW I GOTTA SKIP TOWN BEFORE SOME VERY ANGRY MONKEYS TEAR MY FACE OFF!
GRRRR!
DETENTION, EVERY DAY, FOR THE REST OF YOUR LIFE, NATE! DO YOU HEAR ME?!
THE REST OF YOUR LIFE!
PIMPLE, PIMPLE, WHY HAVE YOU FORSAKEN ME?!

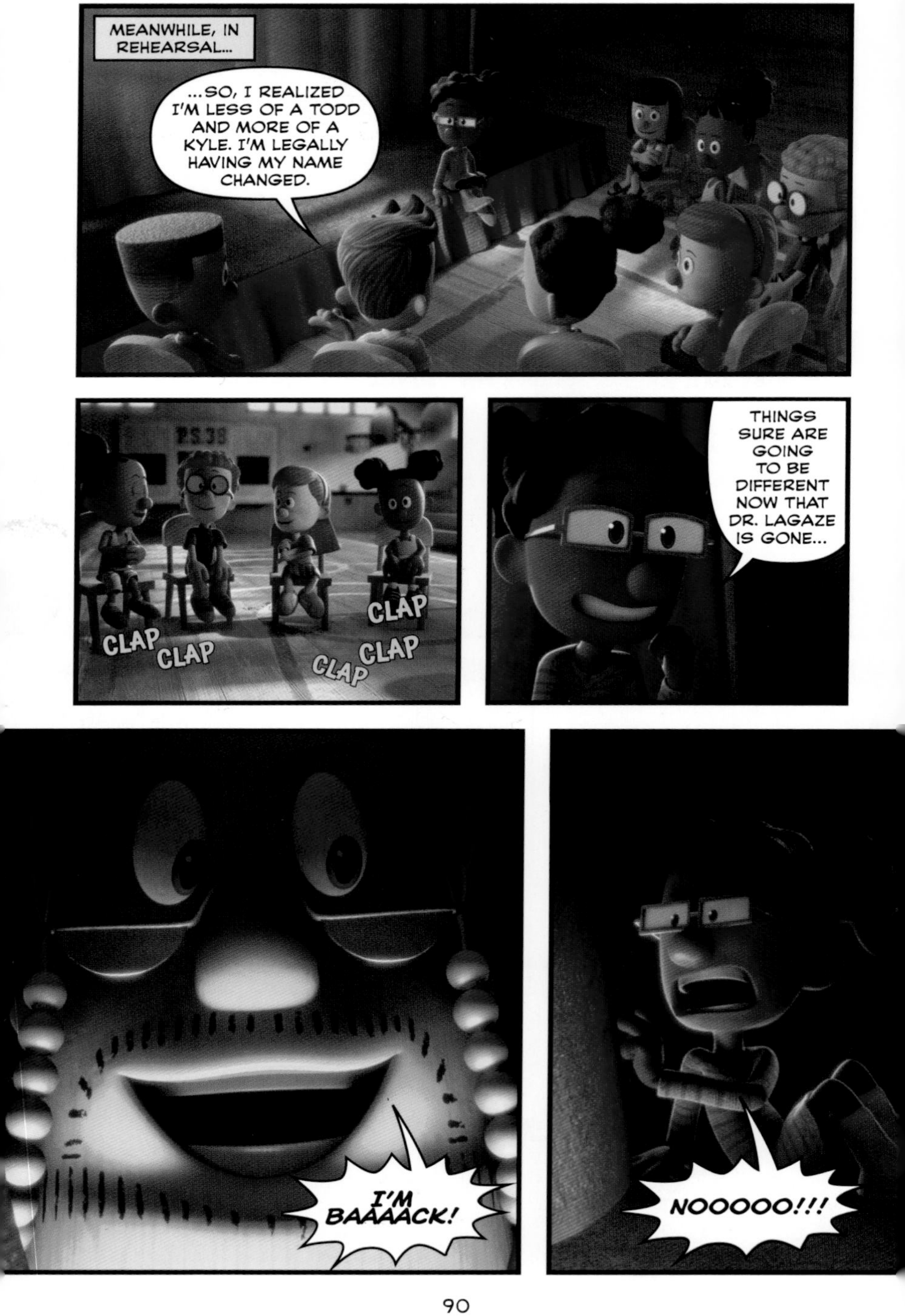
MEANWHILE, IN REHEARSAL...
...SO, I REALIZED I'M LESS OF A TODD AND MORE OF A KYLE. I'M LEGALLY HAVING MY NAME CHANGED.
P.S. 38
CLAP
CLAP
CLAP
CLAP
CLAP
THINGS SURE ARE GOING TO BE DIFFERENT NOW THAT DR. LAGAZE IS GONE...
I'M BAAAACK!
NOOOOO!!!

YOU KNOW, I CAN HEAR YOU, DEE DEE.
WHAT HAPPENED TO YOUR MOVIE?
CREATIVE DIFFERENCES, MY DEAR. THOSE HOLLYWOOD AMATEURS DIDN'T UNDERSTAND MY GENIUS!
TELL ME ALL OF YOUR TIME-TRAVELING SECRETS, TIME DISRUPTORS...
FWIP!
...BEFORE I, EVIL THOMAS EDISON, CONDUCT ELECTRICITY THROUGH YOU!
SPLAT!
WHAM!
CUT!
HEY, DOES ANYONE ELSE SMELL BANANAS?
SIGH.

WE'LL START RIGHT WHERE WE LEFT OFF. EVERYONE TAKE OUT YOUR "DEATH OF A SAILORMAN" SCRIPTS.
WE THREW THEM AWAY!
WHAT? WHO?
WHERE? WHEN?
...WHYYYYYY???
BECAUSE IT WAS HACKY AND UNINSPIRED. WE WANT SOMETHING *REAL!*

WOOO! YES!

ENOUGH OF THIS CODSWALLOP! TAKE OUT YOUR DRAMATIC PRODUCE!

BOOOO!
AH! OW! OOOH!

Chapter 4
THE POP
GET HIM!
WA-W- WAIT! STOP, STOP! LOOK, EVERYBODY, I'M SORRY YOUR LUCK CHANGED! I AM! BUT DON'T BLAME ME!
BLAME THE PIMPLE!
YOU HEARD THE BOY! DESTROY THAT PIMPLE!
BUT HOW DO YOU DESTROY A PIMPLE?
DUH! YOU POP IT!

AHHH! WHAT AM I GOING TO DO?! WHERE AM I GOING TO GO?!
FWOOP!

CRRRSH!
WHAM!
PHEW!
MY BABY REVERTED BACK TO CRAWLING!
LOOK AT THIS! PATHETIC.

HOLD STILL. THIS WILL ONLY HURT A BIT...I THINK!

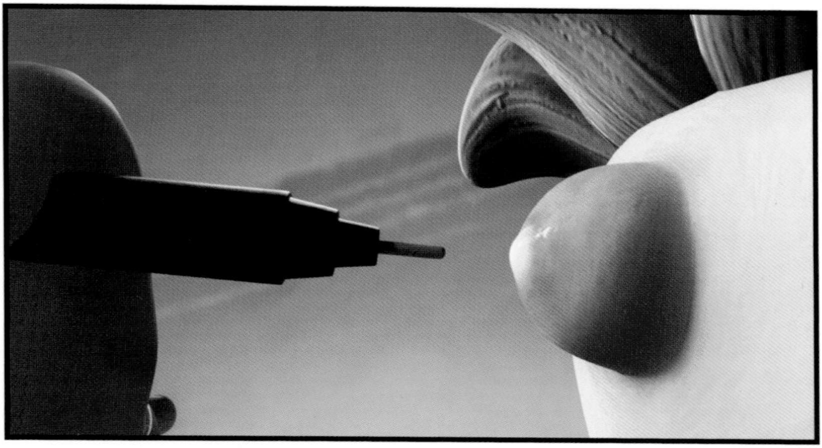

AHHHH!
WHAM!

NATE, IN HERE!

TEDDY, I CAN'T THANK YOU ENOUGH!

IT'S SUPER SCARY OUT THERE!

WHAT ARE YOU DOING?

SORRY, BROTHER, I CAN'T GO TO THAT LAME SUMMER CAMP FOR BRAINIACS. I'M NOT CUT OUT FOR THAT KIND OF TIME.
HE'S IN HERE, GUYS!
GASP! ET TU, TEDDY?
GASP!

HAHAHAHA!
DON'T DO IT, NATE!
UH, YEAH, I'M GONNA DO IT.
OH, HEY KIDS! DON'T WORRY, THAT GREEN GAS IS NONTOXIC AND HUMANELY SOURCED FROM ORGANIC GAS FARMS!
POOF!

CRRRSH!

ZORA, WHAT'S UP? I THOUGHT WE WERE GOOD!
NOBODY USES ZORA'S PIZZA AS ACNE CREAM!
AHHHHH!
NOOOOOOO!

WAIT. WHY ARE YOU HELPING ME? DIDN'T YOUR AWFUL DRAMA TEACHER WHO YOU HATED COME BACK?
HE DID, BUT BECAUSE OF DONNA, I WAS **FINALLY** ABLE TO STAND UP TO HIM!
COME ON, LET'S GO!
WAIT, WHO'S DONNA?

IT'LL ALL BE COVERED IN MY NEW ONE-WOMAN PLAY, "DEE DEE'S DETOURS"!
HURRY! THEY'RE ON OUR TAIL!
HE WENT THATAWAY!
SCREECH!
HEY, WAIT, THIS IS JUST A ***WALL!*** THERE HE IS!

FWIP!
LOOK, I KNOW THIS SEEMS A LITTLE EXTREME...BUT IF I LET THESE ***MANIACS*** POP MY PIMPLE, ELLEN SAID SOMETHING ***TERRIBLE'S*** GONNA HAPPEN!

OH?
YIKES!
GIVE UP, NATE WRIGHT.
WHOA!
HI, NATE! SORRY I'M LATE FOR THE ANGRY MOB.

SURRENDER YOUR PIMPLE, AND WE CAN END THIS SILLY, LEGALLY TROUBLING GAME!

HEY, MOVE ASIDE! MAKE WAY, BEEF-HEADS. BIG SISTER COMING THROUGH.

GET AWAY FROM MY BROTHER!
ELLEN?

WHY, IT'S ELLEN WRIGHT! THE MOST ***EXEMPLARY*** STUDENT TO EVER GRACE P.S. 38'S HALLS!
LOOK AT ALL OF YOU. YOU'VE TURNED INTO SAVAGES. AND OVER WHAT? A ***PIMPLE!***
I USED TO LET PIMPLES RUN MY LIFE.
THEY MADE ME FEEL LIKE A LOSER AND A FREAK...UNTIL I REALIZED THAT I WAS ***MORE*** THAN MY PIMPLES.
YES, THIS SO-CALLED "LUCKY PIMPLE" TURNED MY IDIOT BROTHER INTO AN EVEN ***BIGGER*** IDIOT, BUT WHO HASN'T HAD THEIR OWN INNER PIMPLE DEMONS TO CONQUER?

THEY DON'T CALL THEM "THE DEVIL'S FACE MUSHROOMS" FOR NOTHING!

AND FURTHERMORE, IF ANYONE IS GOING TO POP THIS DWEEB'S PIMPLE...
...IT'S ME!
NO, NO, NOOOOOO!

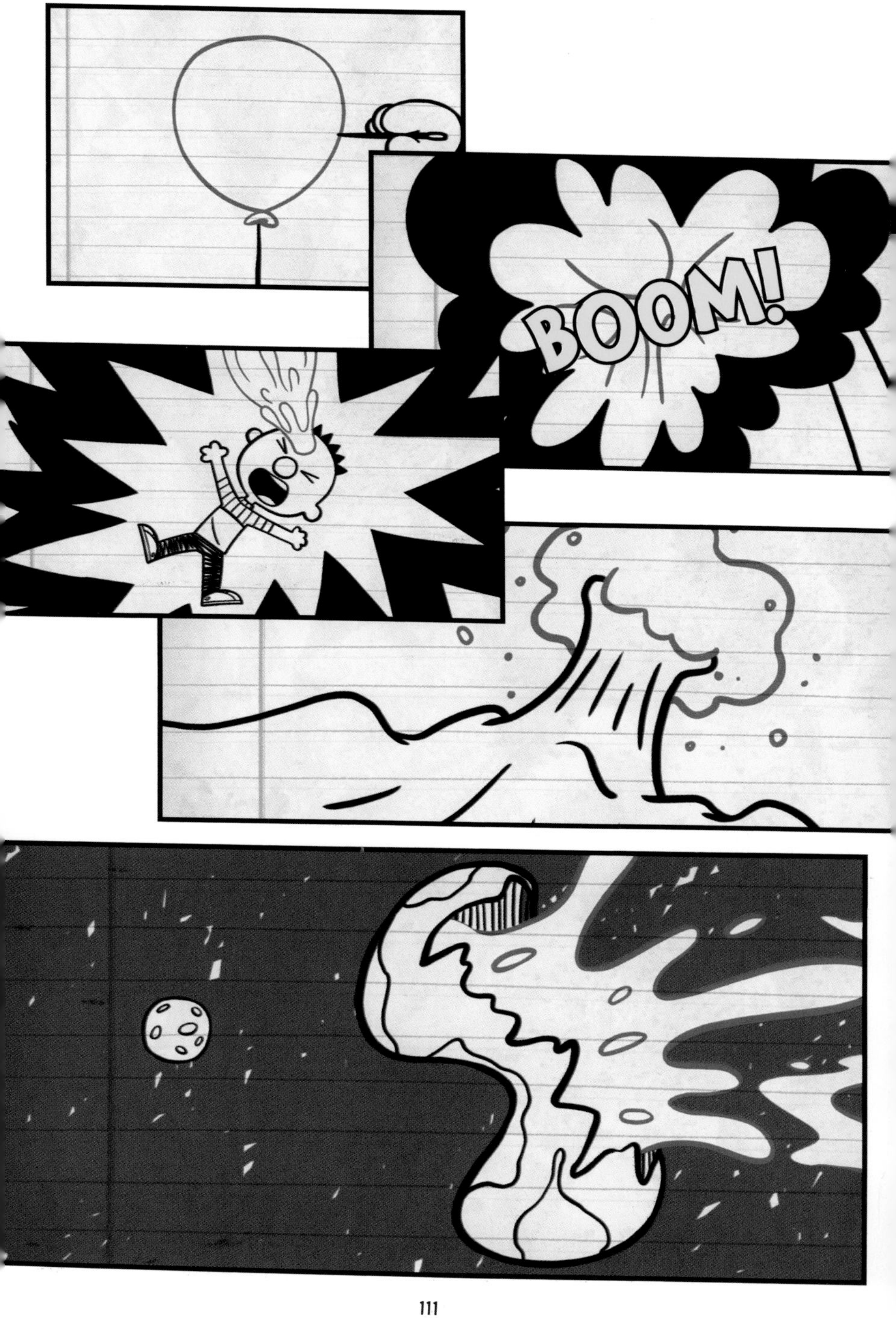
BOOM!

AHHHHH! WHOA, NOTHING BAD HAPPENED?
I WAS JUST MESSING WITH YOU, DORK.
WOOHOO!
YAYYY!
THE THINGS I DO FOR THIS FAMILY.

"AND SO I LEARNED THAT FAME IS FLEETING...
≶YAWNNN!≶
"...ONE DAY, YOU'RE A FAMOUS PIMPLE SHAMAN, THE NEXT DAY, YOU'RE JUST AN ORDINARY–
"–I GOT ANOTHER ONE!"
THIS TIME, I THINK I'M GONNA CHARGE!

I GOT A NOTHING-BURGER OF A PART IN THE SCHOOL PLAY!
YOU KNOW WHAT YOU NEED, DEE DEE? SOME ZIT LUCK!
THIS HONKIN' PIMPLE BRINGS GOOD FORTUNE TO ANYONE WHO TOUCHES IT! IT'LL TURN YOUR LUCK AROUND...
...FOR A PAYMENT OF ONLY FIVE DOLLARS!
YOU'RE CHARGING ME?
TELL YOU WHAT. WE'RE FRIENDS, SO I'LL KNOCK OFF THE SALES TAX.

COMPOSITION
NATE FILES
WIDE RULE
Picture Day

"THIS IS ME."
WELL, IT'S **SUPPOSED** TO BE ME. I'M ANOTHER SAD VICTIM OF PICTURE DAY— AN INSTITUTION RIGGED—
—RIGGED, I TELL YOU!—TO MAKE KIDS LOOK THEIR ABSOLUTE ***WORST!***
HI, LOSER NATE.
HI, ***BUTT-BRAIN GINA.***

AS I WAS SAYING, EVERY YEAR, I DREAD GETTING MY YEARBOOK...BUT NOT THIS YEAR!
THIS YEAR'S GOING TO BE DIFFERENT.
Y'KNOW WHY? BECAUSE I'M ***AWESOME!***
AND BECAUSE I'VE GOT A PLAN...
DOOT-DA-DOO...
STEP ONE: STEAL MR. ROSA'S KEYS!

OM NOM NOM!

I'M NOT JUST DOING THIS FOR MYSELF, MIND YOU.
I'M DOING THIS FOR FRIENDS LIKE CHAD!

SPLOT!

THERE'S SOMETHING IN HIS SCRAMBLED BRAIN THAT CAUSES HIM TO TAKE ILL-ADVISED FASHION RISKS!

SPICY

e Anderson
Chad Applewhite
Adriana D

NOM NOM NOM NOM!
TODAY IS **WAFFLE TUESDAY**, AND IF MY CALCULATIONS ARE CORRECT, MR. ROSA **SHOULD** BE ENTERING A WAFFLE COMA IN THREE...TWO...
WHAM!
ZZZZZZZ!

MR. ROSA HAS THE KEYS TO THE YEARBOOK ROOM. OKAY, TIME TO GO *STEALTH MODE.*
CLANG!
CLANG!
OOOF!
CLANG!
GOT 'EM!

RRRIIINGGG!
STEALTH MODE, PHASE 2!
Definitely a REAL Water Fountain
Thurs 3:30
BE
FWOOSH!
MY FRIEND TEDDY'S PROBLEM IS THAT HE'S GOT *HORRIBLE* TIMING.

OKAY CHAMP, ON THE COUNT OF THREE, SAY "CHEESE!" ONE...
CHEEEEEEEEEESE!!!
AHHH!
ARGGG!
Ellie Mills
Teddy Ortiz
Nichole Phillips
SIGH! POOR KID.
GASP!

AHH, WATER, WATER, WATER, I *LOVE* WATER!
GLUG! GLUG! GLUG!
PSSSHHH!
AHH! REFRESHING!
PHEW.

AND MY BUDDY FRANCIS? TOO MUCH **PARENTAL INTERVENTION.**
GROAN!
SNIP!
SNIP!
TSSS!
DON'T FORGET YOUR SUNSCREEN!
illips
Francis Pope

UGH, AND DON'T GET ME STARTED ON MY GIRL DEE DEE...
HEY, NATE, WAIT UP!
HUH? AHHHHH!
HEH? HEH?
CAW!
CAW!
AHHHHH!
Adriana Davis
Dee Dee Holloway

ERGH!
GASP! I'M IN!
CHCK!
Definitely a REAL Water Fountain
CLICK!
TIME TO FIX SOME PHOTOS.
PASSWORD:
OKAY, HERE WE GO. PASSWORD...

PASSWORD:
MrRosa
...EH, "MR. ROSA"?
PASSWORD:
NO.
You have 4 attempts remainin
PASSWORD:
YrBook
"YEARBOOK"? NO.
You have 3 attempts remaining
PASSWORD:
PS3
WHAT'S THE PASSWORD...? C'MON, NATE!
PASSWORD:
YOUR FRIENDS ARE ***DEPENDING*** ON YOU!
You have 2 attempts remaining
PASSWORD:
Sleep@Wrk
WARNING!
PASSWORD:
One more attempt and you will be logged out.

MWAHAHA! YOU'LL *NEVER* GUESS THE PASSWORD, LOOOOSER!
OH, RIGHT! GINA'S HEAD OF YEARBOOK.
PASSWORD:
NateWrightIsALoser
"NATEWRIGHTISALOSER."
WELCOME TO THE
YEARBOOK
DATABASE
AND NOW...
...THE MAGIC HAPPENS!

Are you sure you want
to replace all (368) photos?
YES
NO
OH, YES.

TWO WEEKS LATER...
AAAHHHHHHHHHHHHH!
PS38
AAAHHHHH!!!
Gina Hemphill-Toms
AAHHH!!!
I LOOK **RIPPED!**

JUST **LOOK** AT THAT WINNING SMILE!
THIS WILL MAKE A **GREAT** HEADSHOT!
HUH, I DON'T REMEMBER OWNING A MONSTER TRUCK...

GRRRRR! WHO'S RESPONSIBLE FOR THIS?!
Principal Nichols
"THE LEGENDARY NATE WRIGHT"?!
The Legendary Nate Wright!
NAAAATE!

PANT! PANT!
THEY'LL THANK ME LATER!
YOU WON'T GET AWAY WITH THIS, LOSER!
WHY YOU LITTLE SO-AND-SO!

Time Disruptors

Chapter 1
THE LEGEND
PS38
SPACE FOR
MRS.
...AND FINALLY, THE SCIENCE DEPARTMENT IS LOOKING FOR ANY PETS YOU NO LONGER NEED.
THE *TYPE* OF PET DOESN'T MATTER, AS LONG AS IT CAN *RUN!*
SIGH.
THANK YOU FOR THOSE, UH, *INSPIRATIONAL* WORDS, MR. GALVIN.
CRAWLING IS FINE, TOO. JUST AS LONG AS THEY'RE *BREATHING!*

PUSH!
AHHH!
MOVING ON TO MORE ENJOYABLE NEWS...
...IT'S MY PLEASURE TO ANNOUNCE THAT IN CELEBRATION OF ANOTHER YEAR WITHOUT LOSING A SINGLE STUDENT TO HOMESCHOOLING, THIS FALL'S COSTUME BALL THEME IS "THE LEGEND OF THE HOMESCHOOL CORN GIRL."
OOOOOHH!
AAAAAHH!

NOW, FOR THOSE UNFAMILIAR WITH THE LEGEND, DEE DEE HOLLOWAY WILL DANCE OUT THE SAME EXACT WORDS I'LL BE SAYING AS I TELL THE TALE!
"LONG AGO, A GROUP OF CIRCUS FOLK CAME TO RACKLEFF. THEIR STAR ATTRACTION WAS A LITTLE GIRL SAID TO HAVE THE VOICE OF AN ANGEL FROM THE HEAVENS.
FAA! LAAA! LAAA!
"NOW, BECAUSE THESE CIRCUS FOLK WERE ALWAYS ON THE ROAD, THE GIRL HAD TO BE ***HOMESCHOOLED*** ON THE FAMILY BUS.
"ONE EVENING, THE CIRCUS FAMILY DECIDED TO PARK THEIR BUS IN A CORNFIELD, BECAUSE THAT'S WHAT THEM CIRCUS FAMILIES DO.

"BUT SUDDENLY, A FREAKISH STORM SWEPT IN!"
AHHHHHHHH!
FOOOSSHH!
THEY WERE NEVER SEEN AGAIN. LOST FOREVER, IN THE CORNFIELD.
AS LEGEND GOES, HE WHO SEES THE CORN GIRL IS DOOMED...DOOMED... DOOMED...DOOMED...
CORN GIRL! DARK DANCE! CORN GIRL! DARK DANCE!
CORN GIRL! DARK DANCE! CORN GIRL! DARK DANCE!
CORN GIRL!
DEE DEE!!

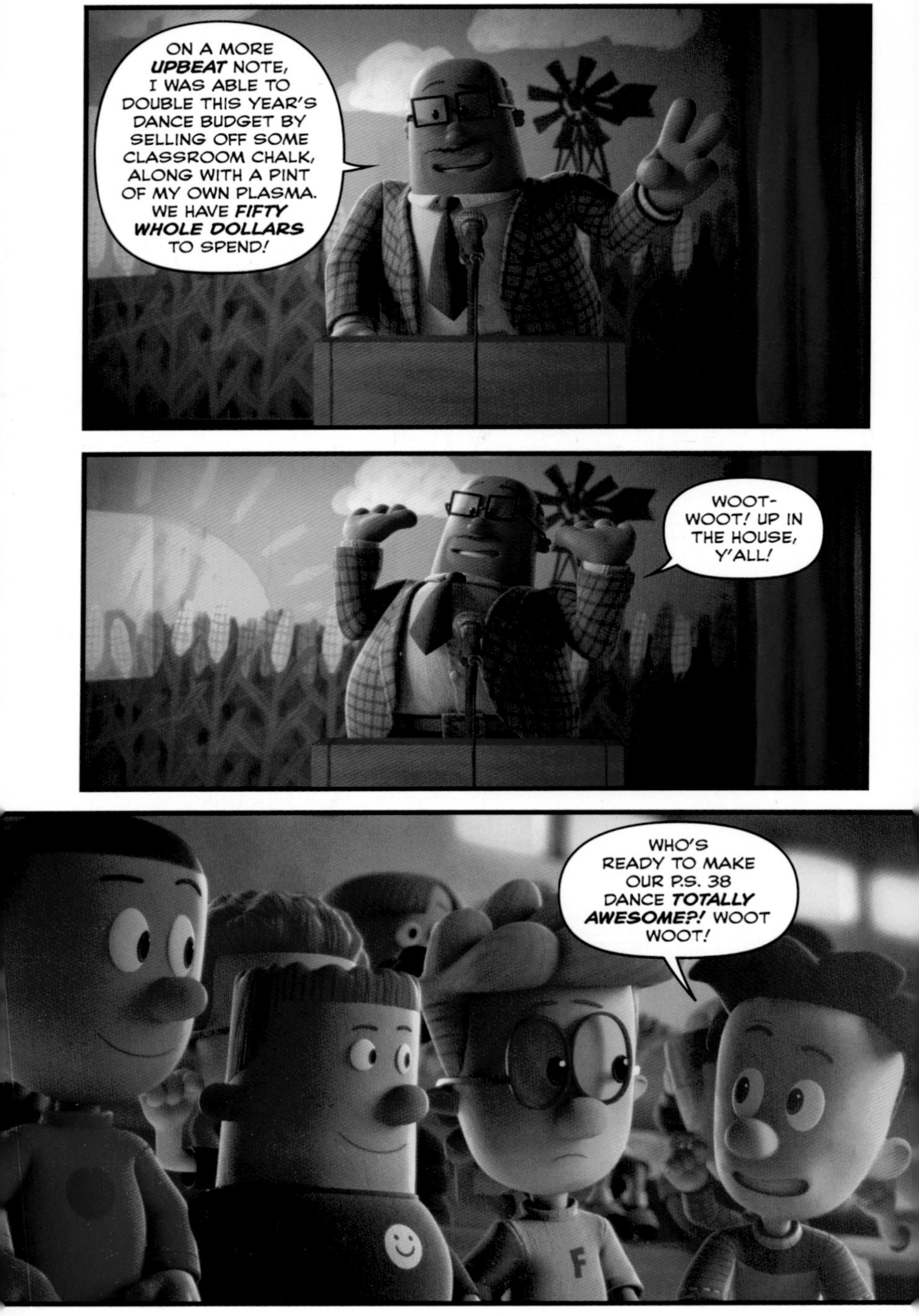
ON A MORE **UPBEAT** NOTE, I WAS ABLE TO DOUBLE THIS YEAR'S DANCE BUDGET BY SELLING OFF SOME CLASSROOM CHALK, ALONG WITH A PINT OF MY OWN PLASMA. WE HAVE **FIFTY WHOLE DOLLARS** TO SPEND!
WOOT-WOOT! UP IN THE HOUSE, Y'ALL!
WHO'S READY TO MAKE OUR P.S. 38 DANCE **TOTALLY AWESOME?!** WOOT WOOT!

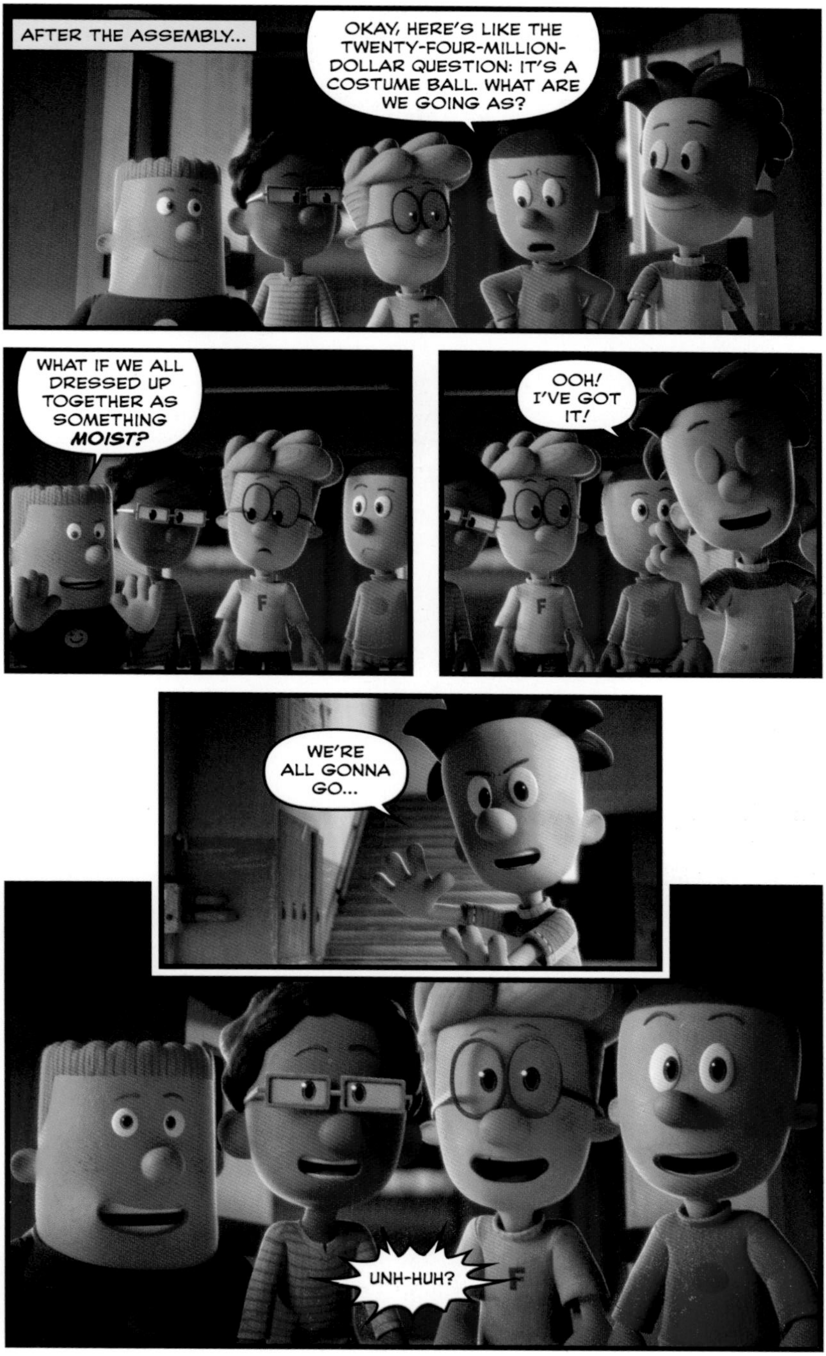
AFTER THE ASSEMBLY...
OKAY, HERE'S LIKE THE TWENTY-FOUR-MILLION-DOLLAR QUESTION: IT'S A COSTUME BALL. WHAT ARE WE GOING AS?
WHAT IF WE ALL DRESSED UP TOGETHER AS SOMETHING *MOIST?*
OOH! I'VE GOT IT!
WE'RE ALL GONNA GO...
UNH-HUH?

AS THE ONE AND ONLY...
UNH-HUH?
TIME DISRUPTORS!
OH MY GOSH, GREATEST IDEA EV-ER!
AHHH!
THAT'S AMAZING!
SO, YOU'RE PROBABLY WONDERING WHO THE TIME DISRUPTORS ARE.
ONLY THE GREATEST ACTION FRANCHISE IN THE HISTORY OF CINEMA!

THE *TIME DISRUPTORS* ARE A GROUP OF SCIENTISTS...
...WHOSE MISSION IS TO BETTER THE WORLD...
...BY CHANGING THE PAST...
...WHICH INEVITABLY MESSES *EVERYTHING* UP IN THE FUTURE...

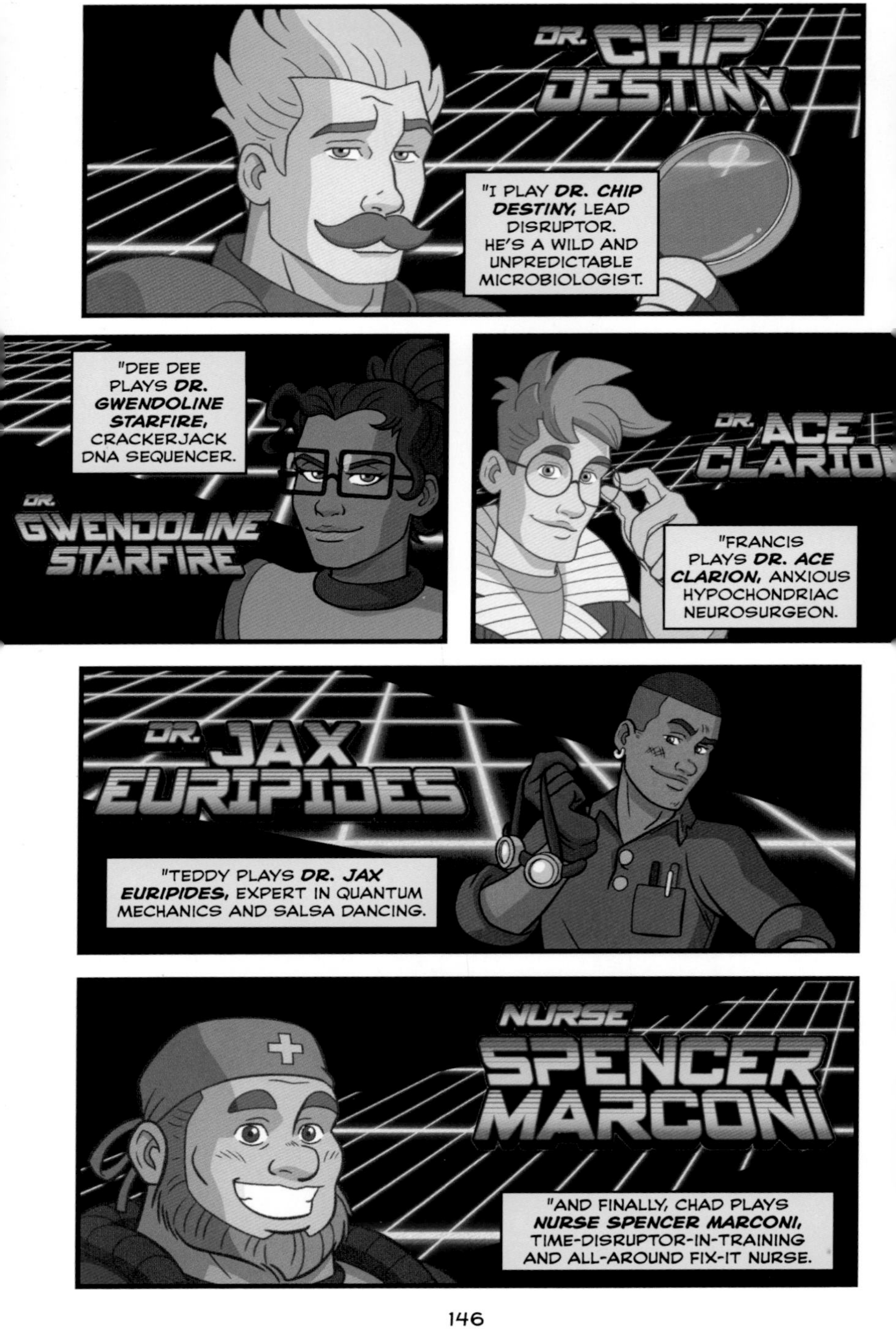
DR. CHIP DESTINY
"I PLAY **DR. CHIP DESTINY,** LEAD DISRUPTOR. HE'S A WILD AND UNPREDICTABLE MICROBIOLOGIST.
"DEE DEE PLAYS **DR. GWENDOLINE STARFIRE,** CRACKERJACK DNA SEQUENCER.
DR. GWENDOLINE STARFIRE
DR. ACE CLARION
"FRANCIS PLAYS **DR. ACE CLARION,** ANXIOUS HYPOCHONDRIAC NEUROSURGEON.
DR. JAX EURIPIDES
"TEDDY PLAYS **DR. JAX EURIPIDES,** EXPERT IN QUANTUM MECHANICS AND SALSA DANCING.
NURSE SPENCER MARCONI
"AND FINALLY, CHAD PLAYS **NURSE SPENCER MARCONI,** TIME-DISRUPTOR-IN-TRAINING AND ALL-AROUND FIX-IT NURSE.

"SO THAT'S US: ***THE TIME DISRUPTORS!***"

WE ARE GOING TO ***OWN*** OUR FIRST-EVER P.S. 38 DANCE!

ANY QUESTIONS?

LATER.
KNOCK! KNOCK!
YOU CALLED FOR ME, PRINCIPAL NICHOLS?
COME IN! GRAB A SEAT.
SO FRANCIS...
THE REASON I BROUGHT YOU HERE TODAY IS THAT THERE'S A GIRL AT JEFFERSON MIDDLE SCHOOL WHO NEEDS A *TUTOR*.
ER... YEAH?

ACCORDING TO...WHATEVER THESE COLORFUL DESIGNS ARE...YOU'RE THE ***SMARTEST*** SIXTH GRADER AT P.S. 38! MAZEL TOV!
CRASH!
DID SOMEONE CALL FOR THE ***SMARTEST*** SIXTH GRADER AT P.S. 38?!

I APPRECIATE THE HUSTLE, GINA, BUT NO, I DEFINITELY DID **NOT** CALL FOR YOU–
MM-KAY. I'LL BE RIGHT OUTSIDE IF YOU DO!
PRINCIPAL NICHOLS, I'VE NEVER TUTORED BEFORE, MAYBE GINA–
NO! GINA IS ***TERRIFYING!*** SHE HAS THE PEOPLE SKILLS OF AN AGGRESSIVE CAR SALESMAN!

OH, FRANCIS, WE NEED THIS TO GO WELL SO PARENTS WILL SEND THEIR KIDS *HERE* INSTEAD OF TO JEFFERSON!
WE'LL GET A TAX BREAK! WE'LL FIX THE KITCHEN! ⋟SOB!⋞
FINE.
FINE?!
THAT'S WHAT I SAID. FINE.
I JUST HOPE MY FRIENDS DON'T FIND OUT I'M HELPING... ***JEFFERSON.***

AFTER SCHOOL.
PS38
IM FAST
HMMM?
VWOOSH!
GRRRRR!

PFF!
PFF!
PFF!
GASP!
CORN GIRL.....

WHOOAA!

Evil!
JEFFERSON MIDDLE SCHOOL
Corporate Funded!
PPPPBTTT!

HELLO?
AHHHHHH!

CRASH!

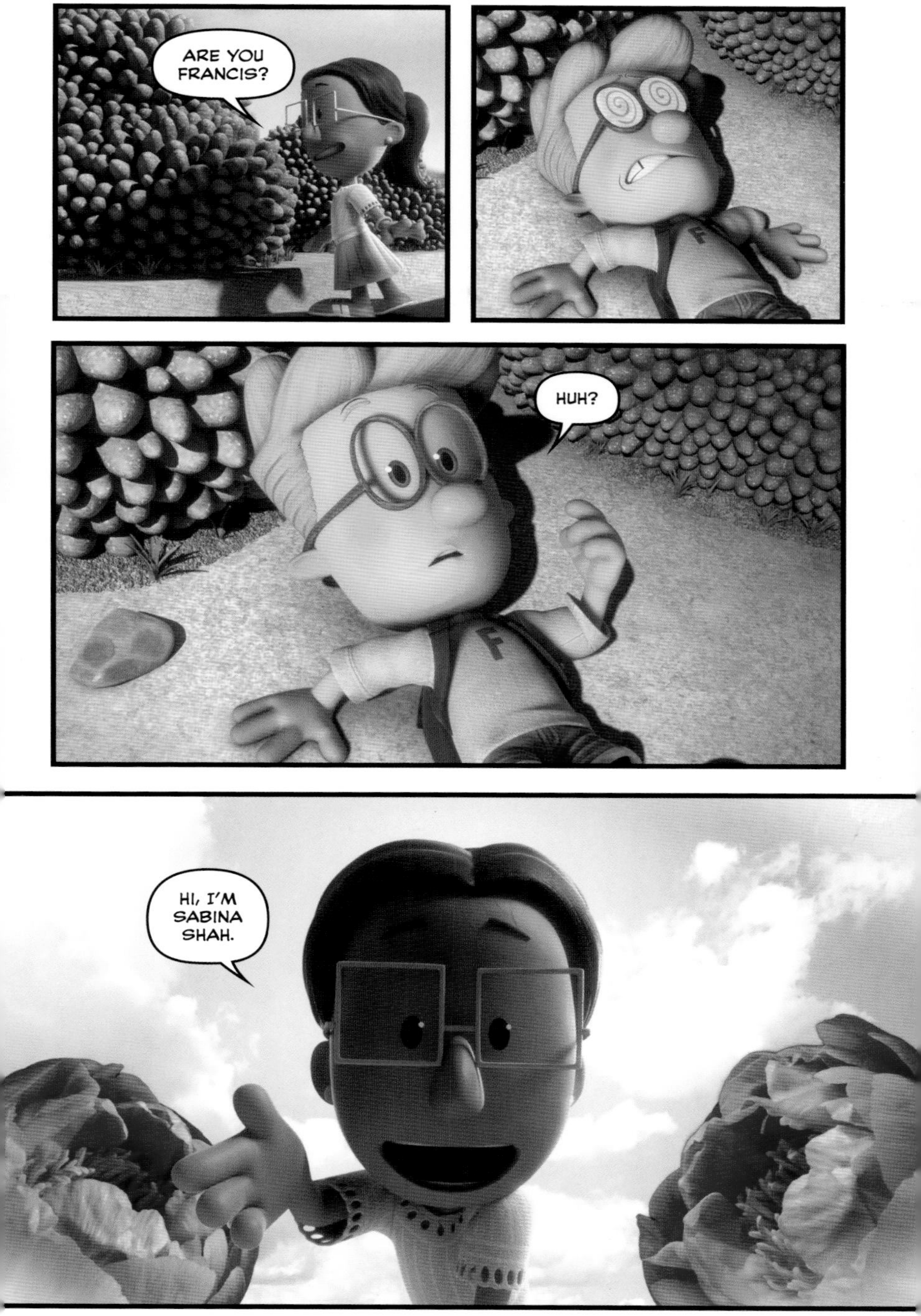
ARE YOU FRANCIS?
HUH?
HI, I'M SABINA SHAH.

NICE JUMP!
GOTTA WORK ON THAT LANDING, THOUGH.
WAIT FOR ME!
HEHEHEHEHE!

Chapter 2
TIME DISRUPTORS, SADDLE UP!
WHERE'S FRANCIS?
NO IDEA! THAT KID HAS BEEN ACTING SQUIRRELY OF LATE.
I LIKE SQUIRRELS!
UHHHH...
DUDE, WHERE'S YOUR ACE CLARION COSTUME?

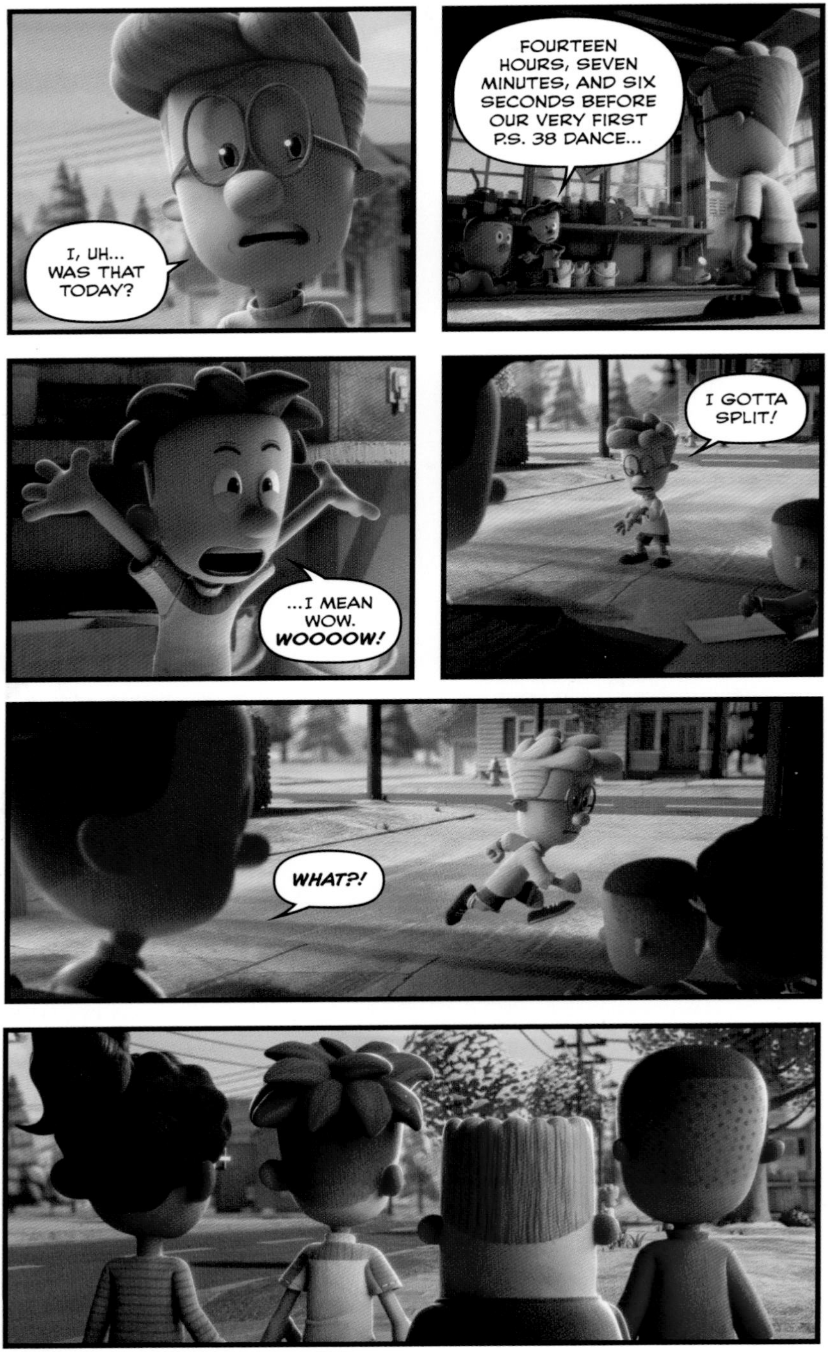
I, UH... WAS THAT TODAY?
FOURTEEN HOURS, SEVEN MINUTES, AND SIX SECONDS BEFORE OUR VERY FIRST P.S. 38 DANCE...
...I MEAN WOW. ***WOOOOW!***
I GOTTA SPLIT!
WHAT?!

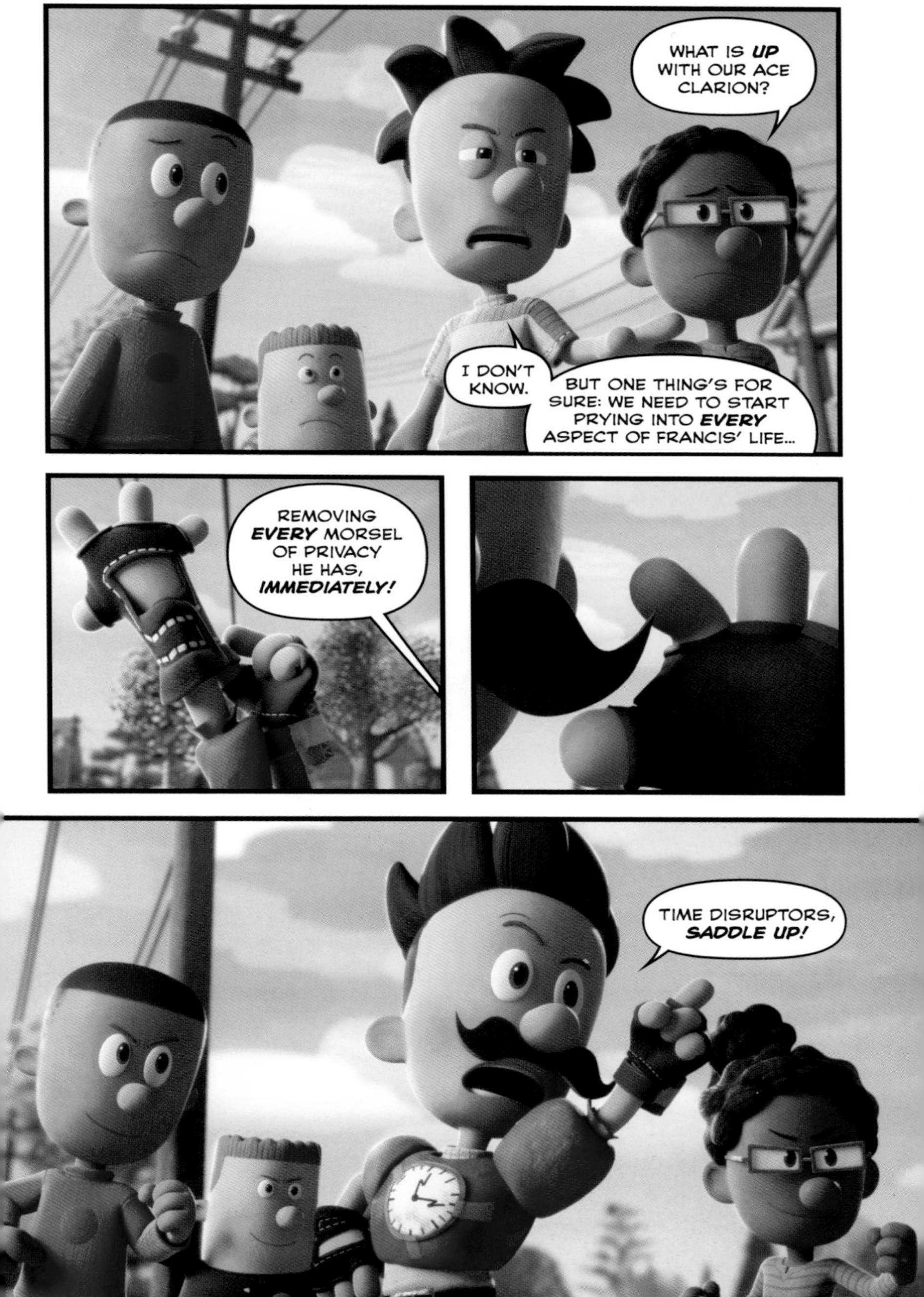
WHAT IS *UP* WITH OUR ACE CLARION?
I DON'T KNOW.
BUT ONE THING'S FOR SURE: WE NEED TO START PRYING INTO *EVERY* ASPECT OF FRANCIS' LIFE...
REMOVING *EVERY* MORSEL OF PRIVACY HE HAS, *IMMEDIATELY!*
TIME DISRUPTORS, *SADDLE UP!*

HMMMM...
WOOF?
SNIF!
SNIF!

AHHHHH!!!
TIME DISRUPTORS, IT IS GOIN' DOWN.
SNAP!
OOF!
WHAM!

GASP! LOOK!
THERE'S FRANCIS!
GASP!
WHY IS HE GOING TO ***JEFFERSON?***
LOOKS LIKE WE'LL BE HEADING INTO ***ENEMY TERRITORY!***

EH?
HMM?
WHOA!
THEIR SCHOOL IS IN HEAVEN?!
IT IS SO SHINY!
THIS MUST HAVE COST MONEY!
THIS IS THE PRETTIEST SCHOOL I HAVE EVER SEEN!

JEFFERSON CHARTER
PRESENTS:
LET THEM EAT CAKE
MASQUERADE
BALL
HUH? JEFFERSON IS HAVING THEIR ***OWN*** MASQUERADE BALL...
...ON THE EXACT SAME DAY AS ***OUR*** COSTUME BALL!
WHAT'S A "MASQUERADE"?
IT'S SNOB FOR "COSTUME."
TARGET ***IDENTIFIED!***
HANG ON, TIME DISRUPTORS, I GOT THIS!

LOOKS LIKE OUR TARGET HAS COMPANY!
IS HE TALKING TO...A GIRL?
EW, I THINK THEY'RE ***READING*** TOGETHER. OH, I'M GOING TO BE SICK!
IS FRANCIS TUTORING... GASP!...THE ***ENEMY?!***
IS ***THAT*** RIGHT?

CLOSE. THE IDEA IS TO USE GEOMETRIC NETS TO FIND THE SURFACE AREA OF FIGURES.
OH. SO, WOULD A NET LIKE *THIS* WORK?
5
5
5
5
I, UH, I DON'T SEE WHY NOT. LET ME JUST MAKE A FEW ADJUSTMENTS.

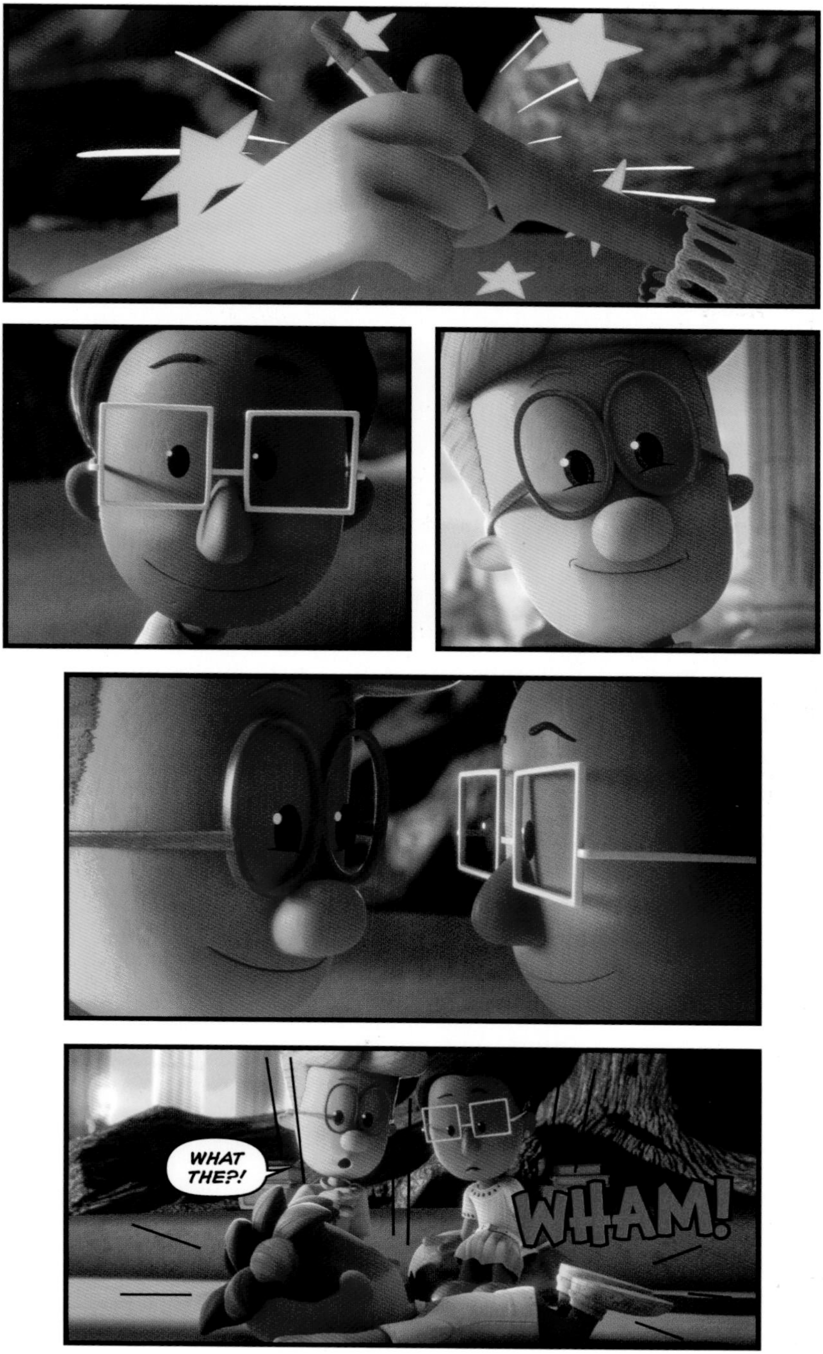
WHAT THE?!
WHAM!

ROLL!
ROLL!
ROLL!
NATE, WHAT ON EARTH?!
SILENCE, *TREASONOUS BUTT-BRAIN!*
FRANCIS, WHAT'S GOING ON?!

HOW COULD YOU GIVE AWAY P.S. 38'S TOP SECRETS?
THE ONLY SECRETS I'M GIVING AWAY ARE GEOMETRY TIPS!
AHHHHH-HAAA!
WAIT, WHAT?
WE'RE DOING HOMEWORK!
≥SNORT!≤ SHE'S TRYING TO DRAIN YOUR BRAIN, FRANCIS!
"SHE" IS NAMED SABINA. AND HOW DOES ONE "DRAIN A BRAIN," PRECISELY?

I CAN SHOW YOU! I JUST NEED A STRAW!
FRANCIS, C'MON, YOU'RE THE **SMARTEST** KID AT P.S. 38! I MEAN, TO JEFFERSON, THAT MAKES YOU **SOLID GOLD**, BABY!
THEY'RE GONNA SUCK THE KNOWLEDGE OUT OF YOU UNTIL THE INSIDE OF YOUR SKULL IS A SAHARAN, BUTT-BRAIN DESERT!
TRUTH. HAPPENED TO A FRIEND OF MINE...KID WAS NAMED CHAD.
⋟GIGGLE!⋞ OOOOH, LOOK AT IT!
JINGLE!

WAIT A MINUTE...IT'S JUST LIKE THE PLOT OF THE TIME DISRUPTORS' CLASSIC, ***"CRISIS ON PLANET BRAIN"!***
SABINA, I'M SORRY, ABOUT... ALL OF THIS.
NO, ***I'M*** SORRY. I DIDN'T THINK YOU TUTORING ME WAS SUCH A BIG DEAL.
IT'S NOT. CAN I CALL YOU LATER?

PRINCIPAL NICHOLS IS MAKING ME TUTOR SABINA. IT'S NOT A BIG DEAL!
OKAY. APOLOGY ACCEPTED! AND, HEY, MAYBE THERE'S A SMALL POSSIBILITY I GOT A LITTLE CARRIED AWAY IN THERE.
SNORT! A "SMALL POSSIBILITY"?
YOU WENT FULL HISSY FIT, NATE!
UH, HELLO?! HAS EVERYONE FORGOTTEN THE MISSION? FIRST DANCE AT P.S. 38?
RING A BELL? GREATEST NIGHT OF OUR LIVES?
FRANCIS IS A TIME DISRUPTOR! YOU NEED FIVE TO MAKE IT WORK!
I GET IT! BUT YOU HAVE TO TRUST ME, SABINA IS JUST A GIRL I'M TUTORING. NOTHING MORE!

BUT THAT'S NOT TRUE, THERE'S SOMETHING ABOUT HER, I CAN'T EXPLAIN...
...A FEELING INSIDE I CAN'T CONTAIN.
CHARTER SCHOOL GIRL, CHARTER SCHOOL GIRL, I WISH YOU WENT TO PUBLIC SCHOOL.
CHARTER SCHOOL GIRL, CHARTER SCHOOL GIRL, THAT LOTTERY SYSTEM SURE IS CRUEL.
CHARTER SCHOOL GIRL, CHARTER SCHOOL GIRL, I KNOW I MAY SOUND LIKE A FOOL.
...BUT THAT'S ME, I ALSO DROOL.

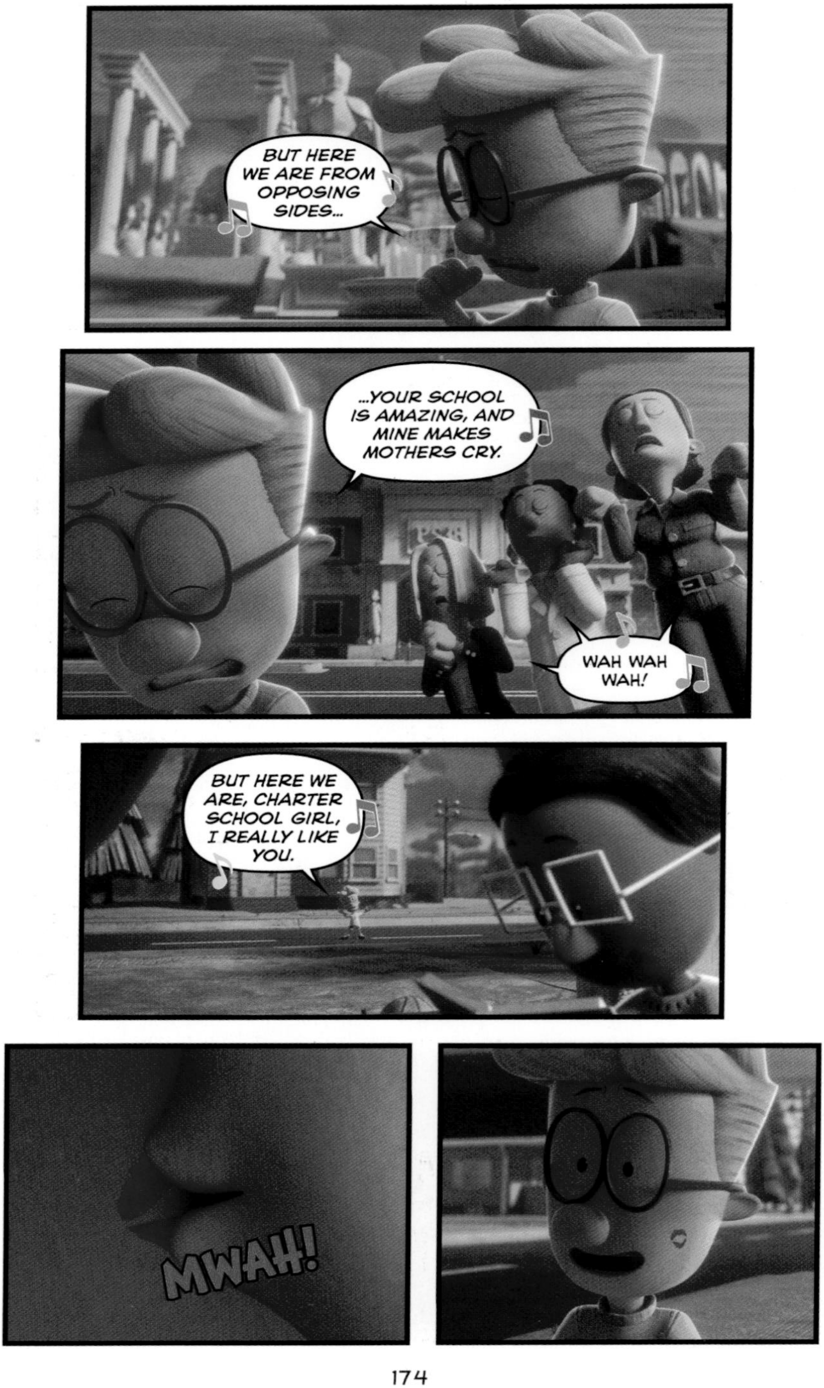
BUT HERE WE ARE FROM OPPOSING SIDES...
...YOUR SCHOOL IS AMAZING, AND MINE MAKES MOTHERS CRY.
WAH WAH WAH!
BUT HERE WE ARE, CHARTER SCHOOL GIRL, I REALLY LIKE YOU.
MWAH!

CHARTER SCHOOL GIRL, CHARTER SCHOOL GIRL, I'VE ONLY KISSED MY MOM BEFORE.
CHARTER SCHOOL GIRL, CHARTER SCHOOL GIRL, DON'T MIND MY LIP, IT'S JUST A COLD SORE.
Mom
CHARTER SCHOOL GIRL, CHARTER SCHOOL GIRL, I'LL BE THE BUTTER FOR YOUR LOBSTER THERMIDOR.
...BUT HERE WE ARE, CHARTER SCHOOL GIRL...
...I REALLY LIKE YOU!

EEEK!
AHHHHHH!
STAY AWAY FROM JEFFERSON!

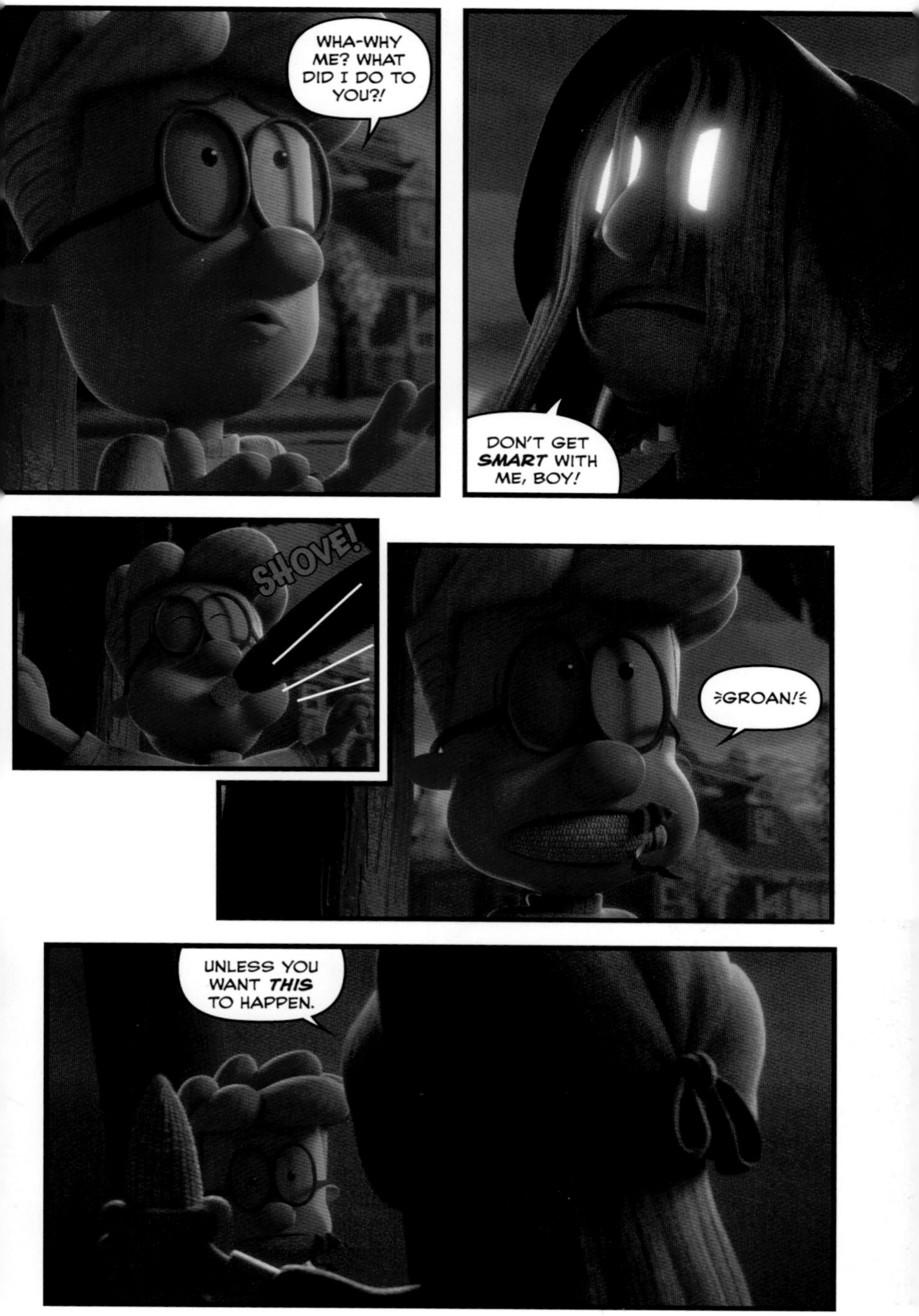
WHA-WHY ME? WHAT DID I DO TO YOU?!
DON'T GET SMART WITH ME, BOY!
SHOVE!
GROAN!
UNLESS YOU WANT THIS TO HAPPEN.

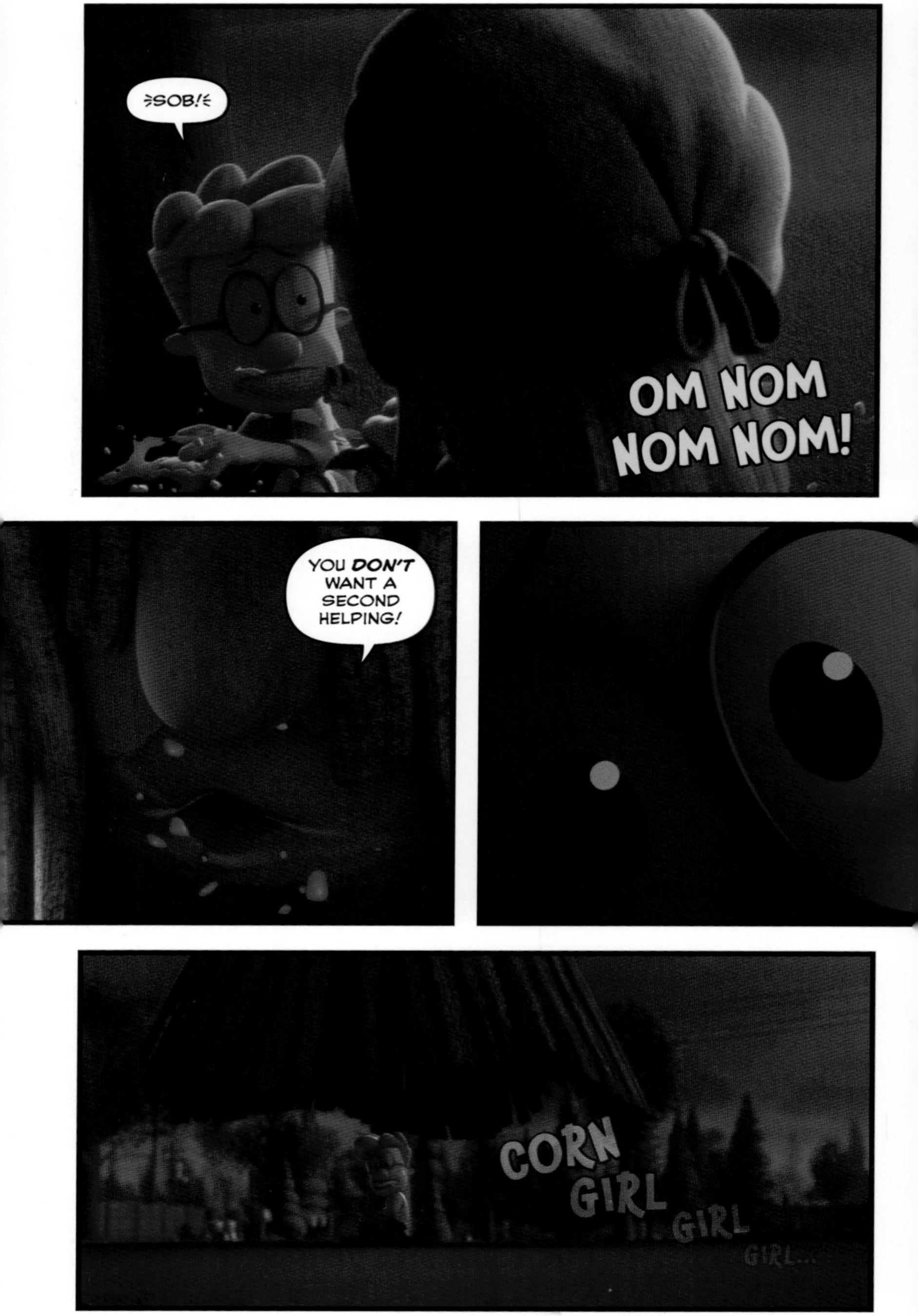
SOB!
OM NOM NOM NOM!
YOU DON'T WANT A SECOND HELPING!
CORN GIRL
GIRL
GIRL...

Chapter 3
ONE LAST MISSION
TIME TO GET DECORATING!
PHOOO
P.S.
S. 38

MEANWHILE AT JEFFERSON.
EEW!

CORN GIRL!
HEY, WANT TO GO TO THIS WITH ME?
JEFFERSON CHARTER PRESENTS:
LET THEM EAT CAKE
MASQUERADE BALL
UMMM...

LATER.
...AND THEN THE CORN GIRL TELLS ME TO STAY AWAY FROM JEFFERSON. ≶GULP!≷ OR ELSE!
WOW, BRO, YOU MUST HAVE DONE SOMETHING TO MAKE HER ANGRY!
BET IT'S YOUR OBSESSIVE FLOSSING!
FLOSS! FLOSS!
I DON'T KNOW WHY YOU'RE FREAKING OUT SO MUCH, FRANCIS.
IF THE CORN GIRL HATES JEFFERSON, THAT MEANS SHE'S ON OUR SIDE!

WELL, LOOK AT THIS, WHAT A NICE SURPRISE!
HAHA. PRINCIPAL NICHOLS, MR. GALVIN, SO GOOD TO SEE YOU...
...HE SAID, *LYING*...
WHAT ARE *YOU* DOING HERE?

WE'RE TRYING TO MAKE UP FOR LOST REVENUE, BUT THESE DECORATIONS AREN'T SELLING DOOR-TO-DOOR.
WOULD ANYONE LIKE TO BUY A BLACK LIGHT POSTER OF YOURS TRULY?
GUYS, I **SERIOUSLY** THINK I'M BLIND!
FRANCIS, MY BOY GENIUS!

I HEAR THINGS ARE GOING SWIMMINGLY!
EVEN GOT YOURSELF AN INVITATION TO THEIR MASQUERADE BALL, EH?
I SMELL A GLUTEN-FREE FRYER IN THE SCHOOL'S FUTURE! WOO-HOO!
GRRR!
NATE, LET ME EXPLAIN!
HMPF!
NATE, TALK TO ME. COME ON, DUDE!

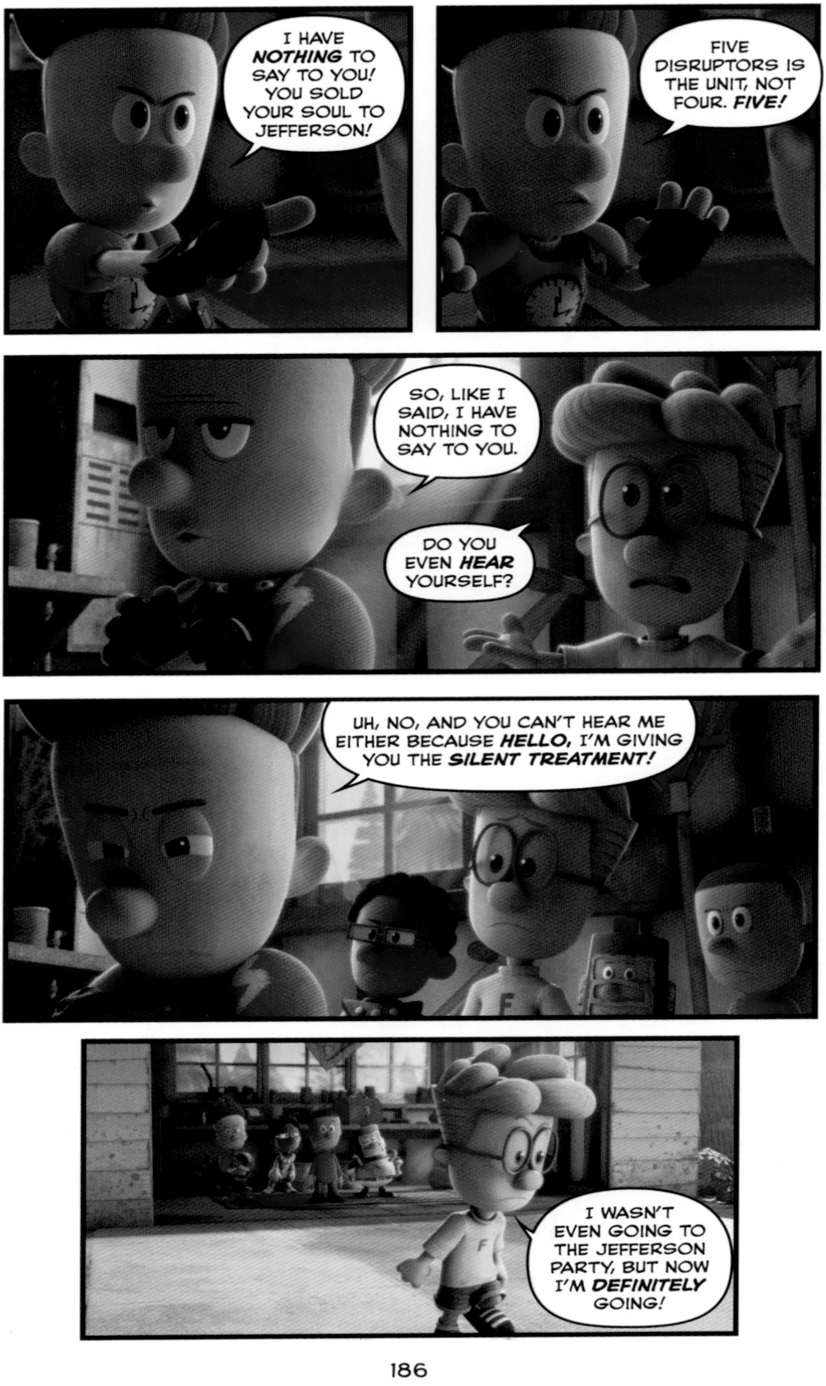
I HAVE NOTHING TO SAY TO YOU! YOU SOLD YOUR SOUL TO JEFFERSON!
FIVE DISRUPTORS IS THE UNIT, NOT FOUR. FIVE!
SO, LIKE I SAID, I HAVE NOTHING TO SAY TO YOU.
DO YOU EVEN HEAR YOURSELF?
UH, NO, AND YOU CAN'T HEAR ME EITHER BECAUSE HELLO, I'M GIVING YOU THE SILENT TREATMENT!
F
I WASN'T EVEN GOING TO THE JEFFERSON PARTY, BUT NOW I'M DEFINITELY GOING!

FRANCIS HAS BETRAYED US FOR JEFFERSON! HE'S ABANDONED THE TIME DISRUPTORS!
I MEAN, HOW ARE WE SUPPOSED TO TAKE CONTROL OF OUR DESTINY NOW?!
LAST TIME I CHECKED, FRANCIS WAS OUR FRIEND.
WHEN ONE TIME DISRUPTOR FALLS, DO WE NOT ALL FALL?
THAT'S IT.
WAIT, THAT'S IT? YOU AREN'T GOING TO ANSWER THAT FALL QUESTION?

HEY, LOOK. DEE DEE'S RIGHT.
THANK YOU, NATE.
NO, NOT ABOUT FRANCIS.
HIS BRAIN HAS *CLEARLY* BEEN DRAINED! BUT HE WAS ONCE A TIME DISRUPTOR, AND WE NEVER LEAVE ONE OF OUR OWN BEHIND, BRAINLESS OR NOT.
TIME DISRUPTORS, *MOUNT UP!*
WE HAVE ONE LAST MISSION TO COMPLETE.

Chapter 4
TAKING CONTROL
OF OUR DESTINY

I FEEL OUT OF PLACE IN THESE CLOTHES!

STOP OVERTHINKING IT. NOBODY'S GONNA NOTICE.

YOU HAVE ***PRECISELY*** TWO SECONDS TO EXPLAIN WHATEVER IT IS YOU THINK YOU'RE WEARING!

UM, WE THOUGHT WE'D GO AS, UH, THE PUBLIC SCHOOL LOSERS FROM ACROSS THE STREET!
HAHAHAHA, NICE ONE! HAVE FUN, KIDDIES!
GUYS, I THINK WE NEED DISGUISES FOR OUR DISGUISES!
TD

GOOD EVENING, MADAM.
AND TO YOU, MY GOOD SIR!
GASP!
ONLY THE TOP 0.1% MAY ENTER

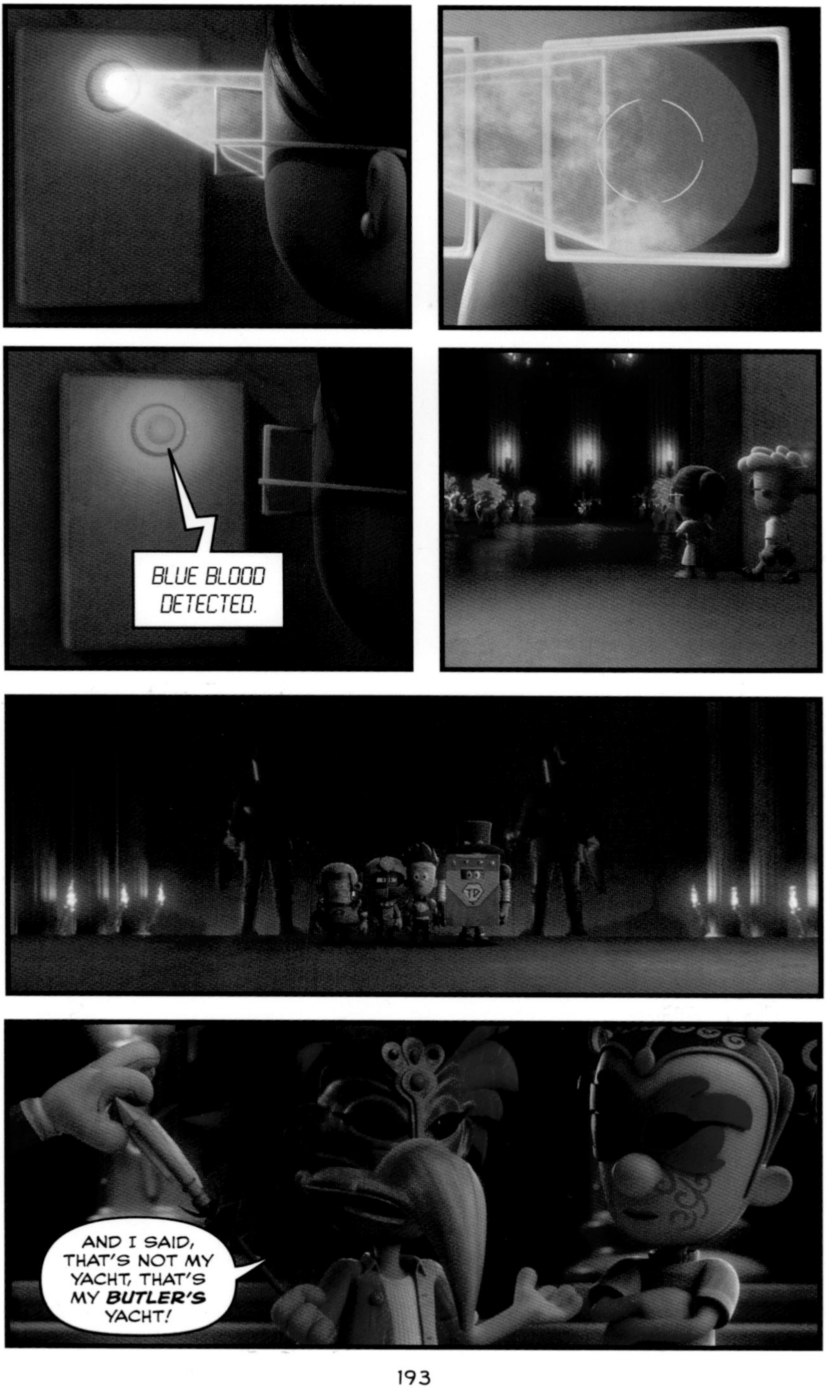
BLUE BLOOD DETECTED.
AND I SAID, THAT'S NOT MY YACHT, THAT'S MY **BUTLER'S** YACHT!

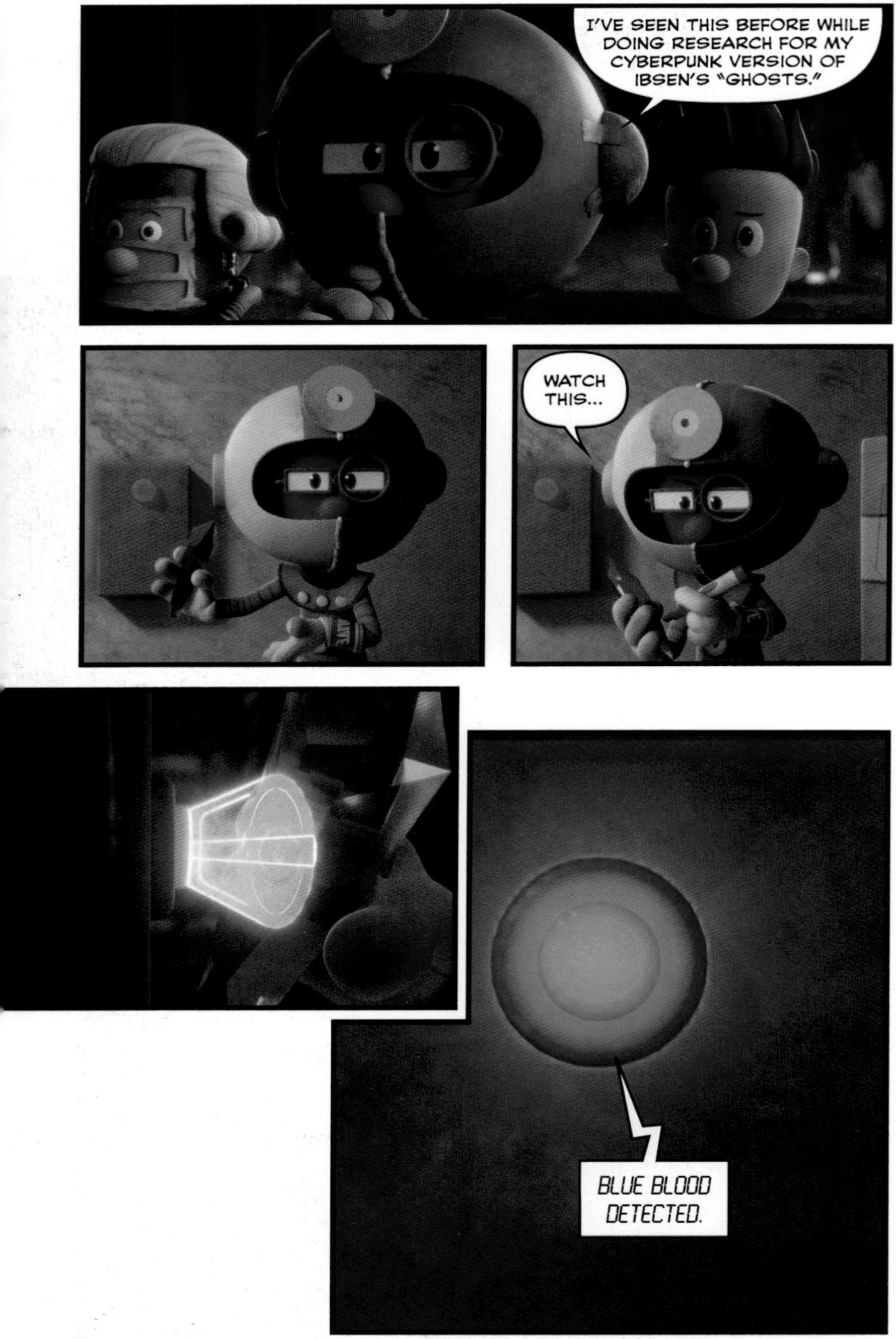
I'VE SEEN THIS BEFORE WHILE DOING RESEARCH FOR MY CYBERPUNK VERSION OF IBSEN'S "GHOSTS."
WATCH THIS...
BLUE BLOOD DETECTED.

ALL RIGHT, GUYS, REMEMBER TO BLEND IN AND THINK RICH!
AY, MAMA!
STATUS IS IN THE SHOULDERS!
IN. THE. SHOULDERS.
HEY! DON'T BE SEDUCED BY THE CHARTER SCHOOL OPULENCE! WE'RE HERE TO SAVE FRANCIS!

LET'S DO THIS!
AND I TOLD MY DAD, I DON'T NEED A *JUMBO* JET! A REGULAR ONE WILL DO JUST FINE.
OM NOM NOM!
WHOA! WOW!

THESE SPIKES ARE EVEN MORE COMFY THAN THE ONES AT HOME!
RATHER PAINTERLY CONSIDERING THE ARTISTS' OEUVRE.
MMM, RATHER BOLD.
HAHA! IN THE WORDS OF VAN GOGH'S SEVERED EAR, SAY *WHAAAT?*
I BEG YOUR PARDON?

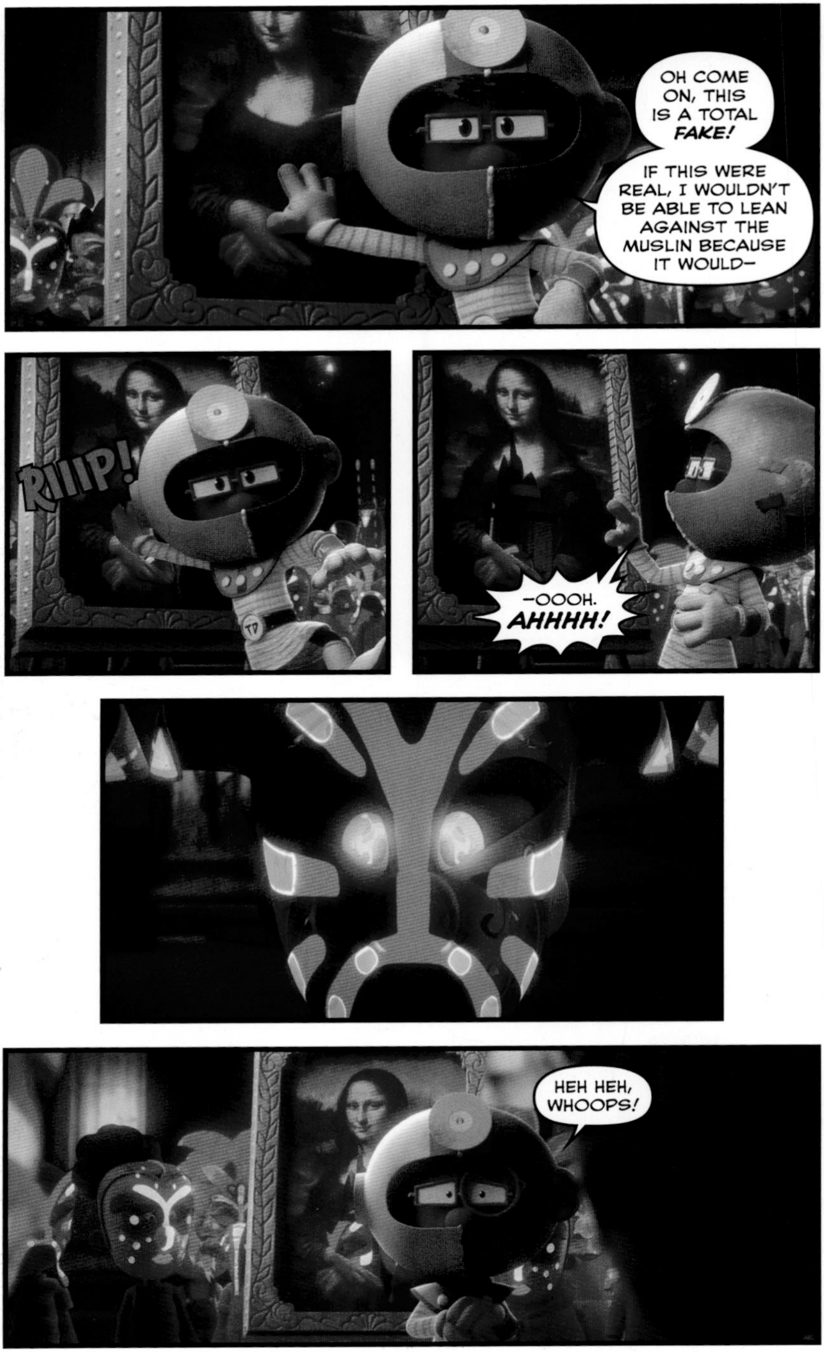
OH COME ON, THIS IS A TOTAL FAKE!
IF THIS WERE REAL, I WOULDN'T BE ABLE TO LEAN AGAINST THE MUSLIN BECAUSE IT WOULD—
RIIIP!
—OOOH. AHHHH!
HEH HEH, WHOOPS!

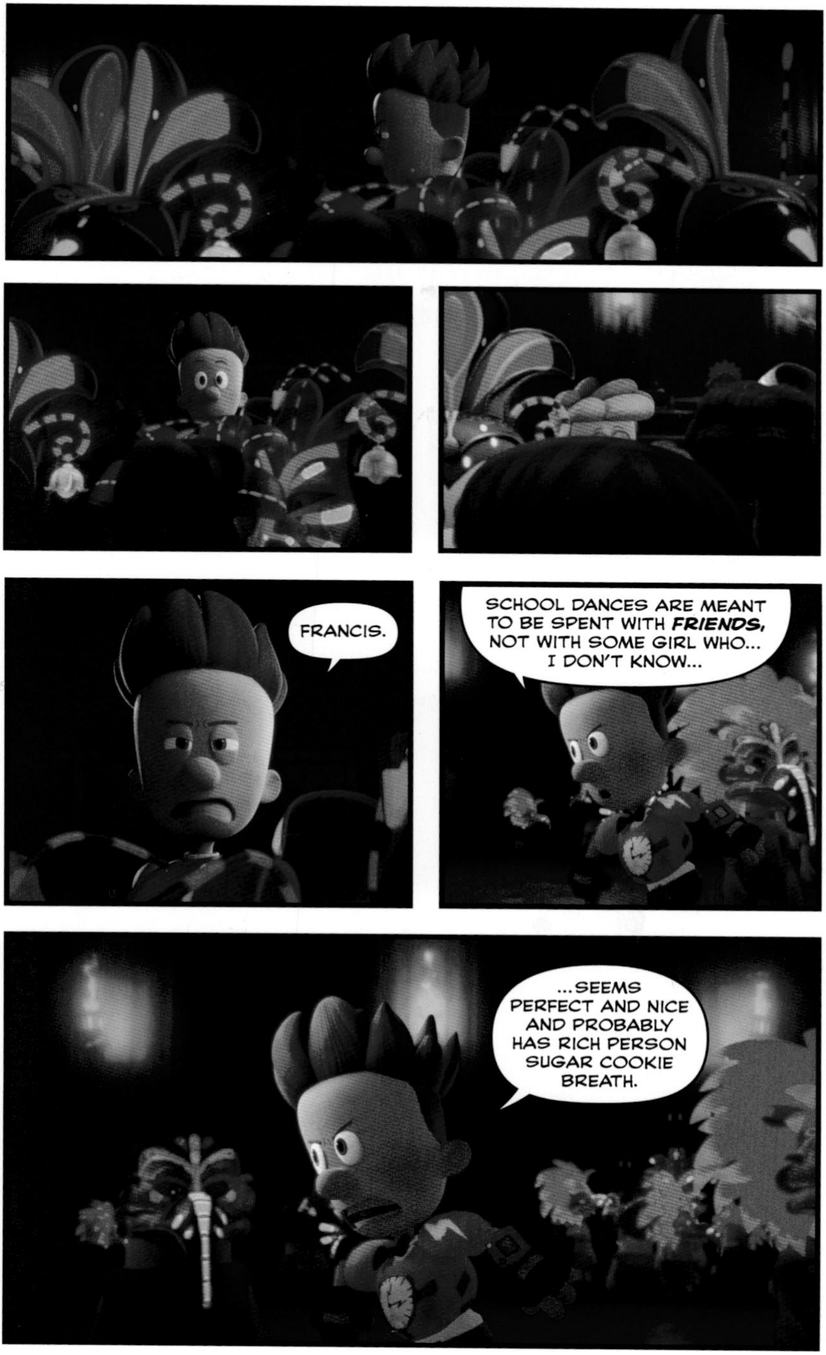
FRANCIS.
SCHOOL DANCES ARE MEANT TO BE SPENT WITH FRIENDS, NOT WITH SOME GIRL WHO... I DON'T KNOW...
...SEEMS PERFECT AND NICE AND PROBABLY HAS RICH PERSON SUGAR COOKIE BREATH.

AND THEN I SAID, THAT'S NOT A LIMA BEAN! BUT YOU SHOULD REALLY GO SEE A DOCTOR.
HAHA!
MWAH!

WOW, FRANCIS LOOKS REALLY HAPPY.
MAYBE COMING HERE WAS TOO... DISRUPTIVE!
CLANG!
AHHH!
CLANG!
CLANG!
CLANG!
WHAM!

CREAK!
CHAD!
SHOO! SHOO!
IF THIS WERE A TIME DISRUPTOR MOVIE, MESSING WITH FRANCIS FINDING HAPPINESS WOULD RESULT IN SOME FUTURE FILLED WITH UNTOLD HORRORS.

NOT AWESOME!

TIME DISRUPTORS, TIME TO DISRUPT TIME ONE MORE TIME!

NOM NOM NOM!

AHHH!
SKID!
AHHHH!
WHAM!
OOMPH!

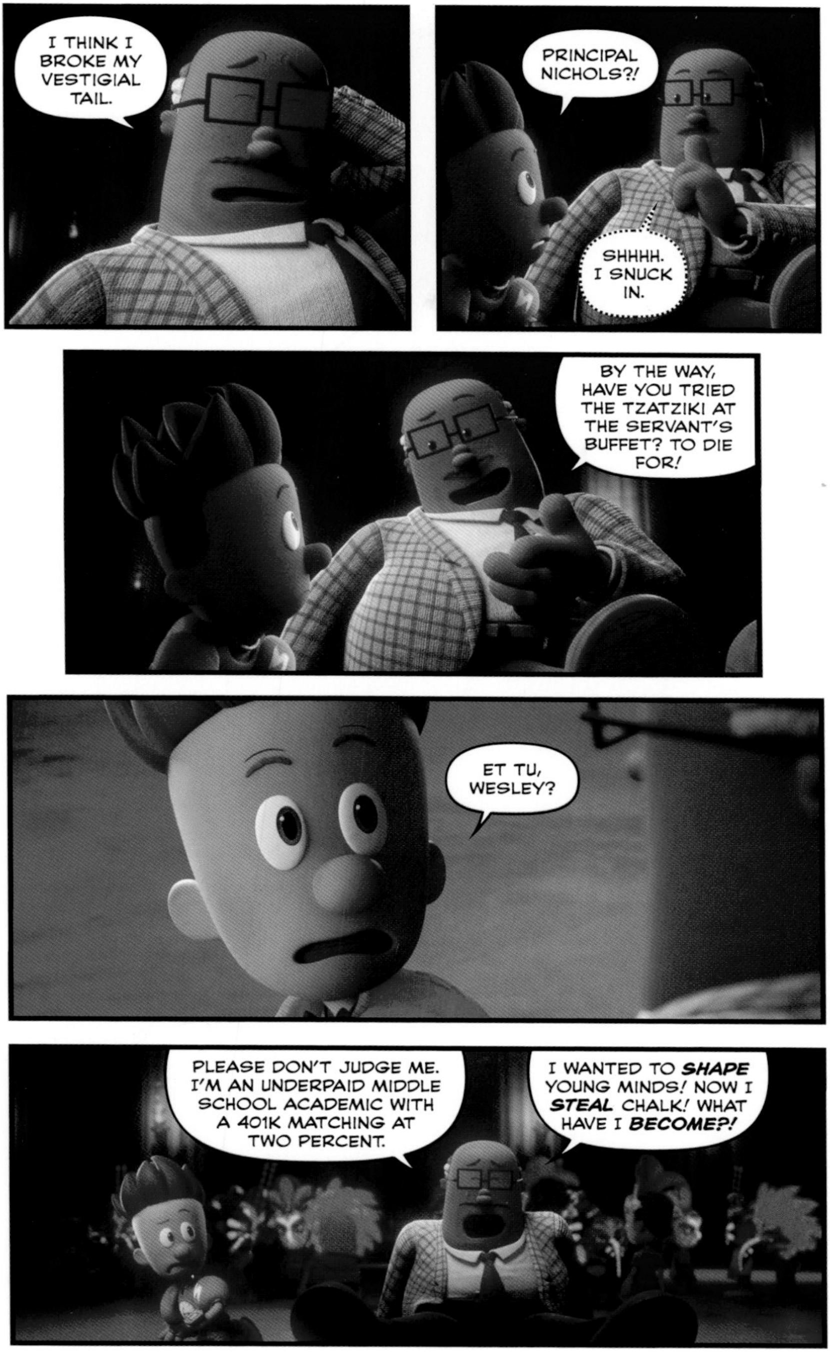
I THINK I BROKE MY VESTIGIAL TAIL.
PRINCIPAL NICHOLS?!
SHHHH. I SNUCK IN.
BY THE WAY, HAVE YOU TRIED THE TZATZIKI AT THE SERVANT'S BUFFET? TO DIE FOR!
ET TU, WESLEY?
PLEASE DON'T JUDGE ME. I'M AN UNDERPAID MIDDLE SCHOOL ACADEMIC WITH A 401K MATCHING AT TWO PERCENT.
I WANTED TO SHAPE YOUNG MINDS! NOW I STEAL CHALK! WHAT HAVE I BECOME?!

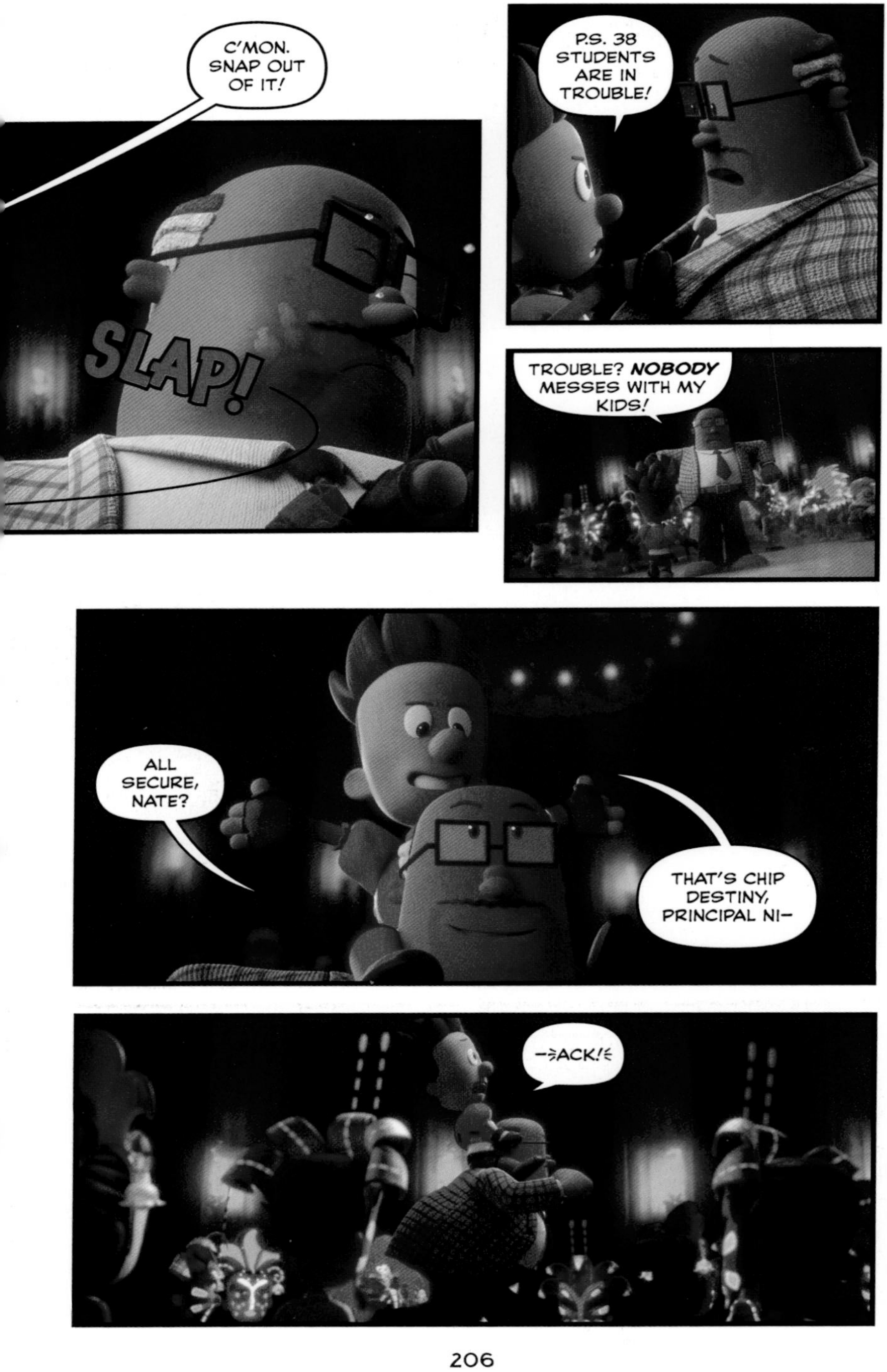
C'MON. SNAP OUT OF IT!
SLAP!
P.S. 38 STUDENTS ARE IN TROUBLE!
TROUBLE? NOBODY MESSES WITH MY KIDS!
ALL SECURE, NATE?
THAT'S CHIP DESTINY, PRINCIPAL NI–
–ACK!

GULP!
GOT YA, CHAD
WHAM!
HUH?!
AAAAHH!!
YOU'RE MINE NOW!
LET'S GO!
WHAM!

C'MON, DEE DEE!
WHERE'D SHE GO?
CLACK!
IF WE DIE, DO THEY AT LEAST BURY US IN THE MAUSOLEUM OUT BACK?

NATE!

YOU CRASHED THE JEFFERSON MASQUERADE BALL?

NO, N-N-NO, IT'S NOT WHAT YOU THINK.

FRANCIS, WHAT IS IT WITH YOU AND YOUR P.S. 38 FRIENDS? YOU'RE LIKE A CULT.
THAT CULT RUMOR WAS NEVER PROVEN!
FRANCIS, THE TIME DISRUPTORS—NO, I—HAD NO RIGHT TO GET MAD AT YOU FOR DOING WHAT MAKES YOU HAPPY!
I KNOW BEING HAPPY FOR YOU ISN'T EASY, BECAUSE OF ALL OF YOUR REALLY INTENSE ISSUES...
WHAT... ISSUES? I DON'T HAVE ISSUES!

I THINK EMOTIONAL FLAWS ARE CUTE!
WOW, IT'S LIKE I CREATED YOU IN A LAB!
ANYWAY, BACK TO ME AND WHAT I'VE LEARNED.
I'VE LEARNED... I'VE LEARNED THE TIME DISRUPTORS ARE FRIENDS FOR LIFE!
BUT YOU'VE ALSO GOT TO LET YOUR FRIENDS HAVE A LIFE!
NOT ME! I AM TOTALLY CODEPENDENT. HEEHEE!
JINGLE!

BOOOO!!!
WHEN ARE YOU PUBLIC SCHOOL CHILDREN GOING TO LEARN YOU'RE NOT LIKE US? CHARTER SCHOOL! HOO-YAH!
CHARTER SCHOOL!
HOO-YAH!
HOO-YAH!

SERIOUSLY, YOU GUYS GOTTA GET OVER YOURSELVES. IT'S A LOTTERY. YOU GOT LUCKY!
TECHNICALLY, IT'S NOT A LOTTERY...
IT'S VOUCHERS!
PUSH!
TRIP!
AHHHHHHH!
FRANCIS!

HANDS OFF! HE'S MINE!
THE HOMESCHOOL CORN GIRL!
YOU! I'M "STALKING" YOU!
GET IT?!

BWA-HA-HA! I WARNED YOU, STAY AWAY FROM JEFFERSON!
NOW EVERYONE'S GOING TO GET CORNED!
RUN!
AHHHHHHH!

AHHH! IT'S THE CORN GIRL!
SHE'S GOING TO CORN US, SHE'S GOING TO CORN US ALL! LET US OUT!

AHHHHH!

HAHAHAHAHA!
I WARNED YOU!

TIME DISRUPTORS... AND SABINA. ON ME!

FRIENDS?
FRIENDS.
AAAHHHHH!
AHHHHH!

AHHHH!!!
AHHHH!!!
WAIT A MINUTE! OUR PARTY IS STILL GOING ON, RIGHT, PRINCIPAL NICHOLS?
YES! AND AS PRINCIPAL, I *SHOULD* PROBABLY GO MAKE AN APPEARANCE.

Y'KNOW, THIS IS STILL OUR FIRST P.S. 38 DANCE! AND WHILE THINGS MAYBE DIDN'T GO AS I'D PLANNED, THAT ***DOESN'T*** MEAN WE CAN'T STILL HAVE FUN...
CLAP!
TAKING CONTROL OF OUR DESTINY! HAHA!
AHHHH!!!

SWIPE!
WHO'S THE SMARTEST KID AT P.S. 38 NOW, FRANCIS!?
BWA-HA-HA-HA-HA!
CORN GIRL...

I CAN'T BELIEVE YOU'RE TUTORING A GIRL FROM JEFFERSON!
I KNEW YOU'D SAY THAT.
WHY TUTOR SOMEONE FROM OUR ARCH-RIVAL? THERE'S PLENTY OF KIDS YOU COULD TUTOR RIGHT HERE!
LIKE WHO? YOU?
ME? NO, WHY WOULD I NEED TUTORING?
ON OUR LAST MATH TEST, YOU GOT A TWELVE.
BUT IT WAS GRADED ON A CURVE, SO I'M GOOD.
Peirce

SHOW CREDITS

WRITTEN BY
MITCH WATSON
ELLIOTT OWEN
SARAH ALLAN
ERIC SHAW

STORYBOARD ARTISTS
KAT CHAN
LAKE FAMA
HEATHER GREGERSEN
KIMBERLY JO MILLS
JIM MORTENSEN
JEFF DEGRANDIS
BRADLEY GOODCHILD
ZOË MOSS
KYLE NESWALD
KEVIN SINGLETON
GREY WHITE
SEBASTIAN DUCLOS
RAY GEIGER
BRANDON WARREN
MARIANA YOVANOVICH
MARIA NGUYEN
MEG SYVERUD
COLIN HECK
MIKE DOUGHERTY
VICTORIA HARRIS
BENJAMIN HOLM
TANNER JOHNSON

CONSULTING PRODUCER
LINCOLN PEIRCE

CO-PRODUCER
BRIDGET MCMEEL

ART DIRECTOR
DAVID SKELLY

CG SUPERVISOR
CHRISTINA LAFERLA

SUPERVISING PRODUCER
JIM MORTENSEN

PRODUCER
AMY MCKENNA

EXECUTIVE PRODUCER
JOHN COHEN

EXECUTIVE PRODUCER
MITCH WATSON
HEAD WRITER
EMILY BRUNDIGE
STAFF WRITERS
SARAH ALLAN
BEN LAPIDES

ASSOCIATE PRODUCER
TAYLOR BRADBURY
STORYBOARD REVISIONISTS
ANDREW CAPUANO
MISTY MARSDEN
JAZZLYN WEAVER

SCRIPT COORDINATOR
LISSY KLATCHKO
PRODUCTION COORDINATORS
BRANDON CHAU
CLAIRE NORRIS
CARLINA WILLIAMS
LOGAN YUZNA
SIENNA SERTL
ASSET PRODUCTION COORDINATORS
DIANA GRIGORIAN
SEAN MCPARTLAND

PRODUCTION ASSISTANTS
CYNTHIA CORTEZ
SARA FISHER
DARREN OJEDA
NATASHA SHIELDS
HANNAH JANE GOULDEN
CAITLYN KURILICH
AJ SHENEFELT
EXECUTIVE ASSISTANT
ALEX VAN DER HOEK

CHARACTER DESIGNERS
ROBERT BROWN
JUN LEE
JOCELYN SEPULVEDA
BACKGROUND DESIGNERS
PETER J. DELUCA
GRACE KUM
BECCA RAMOS
JOSH WESSLING
PROP DESIGNERS
ZACHARY CLARKSON
TYLER WILLIAM GENTRY
RC MONTESQUIEU
SHANNON PRESTON
2D DESIGNER
VICKI SCOTT
BACKGROUND PAINTERS
NATALIE FRANSCIONI-KARP
JONATHAN HOEKSTRA
QUINTIN PUEBLA
PATRICK MORGAN

LEAD CG GENERALIST
VYPAC VOUER
LEAD CHARACTER TECHNICAL DIRECTOR
AREEBA RAZA KHAN
LEAD LOOK DEVELOPMENT ARTIST
CANDICE STEPHENSON
LOOK DEVELOPMENT ARTIST
JUAN GIL

COLOR CORRECTION SERVICES
ROUNDABOUT ENTERTAINMENT
COLORIST
BRYAN MCMAHAN

CG GENERALIST
THOMAS THOMAS III

ANIMATION DIRECTOR
DENNIS SHELBY
MARK LEE
LIGHTING & COMPOSITING DIRECTOR
DARREN D. KINER
CODY BURKE
ASSOCIATE ART DIRECTOR
SAM KOJI HALE

2D ANIMATION SERVICES
XENTRIX TOONS
FOR XENTRIX TOONS
CREATIVE DIRECTOR
HARRIS CABEROY
PRODUCTION MANAGER
SHERYLEN CAOILI
FX SUPERVISOR
KERWIN OJO
PRODUCTION TEAM
ARA KATRIN LUDOVICO
JANILLE BIANCA TUDELA

SPECIAL THANKS
BRIAN ROBBINS
RAMSEY NAITO
BRIAN KEANE
ANGELIQUE YEN
DANA CLUVERIUS
CLAUDIA SPINELLI

ANIMATION DEVELOPMENT
NATHAN SCHRAM
LESLIE WISHNEVSKI

CURRENT SERIES MANAGEMENT
NEIL WADE

VICE PRESIDENT OF ANIMATION PRODUCTION
DEAN HOFF

EXECUTIVE IN CHARGE FOR NICKELODEON
NATHAN SCHRAM

nickelodeon
BiG NATE
NEW SERIES
NOW STREAMING
Paramount+
ORIGINAL
022 Viacom International Inc. All Rights Reserved.

Complete Your *Big Nate* Collection